"Did I tell
desirable?"
roughly.

She slowly shook her head.

"What did I say, Sara?"

She paused uncertainly. "That I was beautiful."

"More than that."

Sara shook her head. "I don't want to hear this."

"Desirable. Beautiful. Sexy beyond belief." He angled his mouth towards hers. "A passionate woman who needs to be kissed. Often."

Welcome to our mini-series **DADDY BOOM**! Just look who's holding the baby! Meet gorgeous heroes who are about to discover that there's a first time for everything—even fatherhood!

This month it's the turn of Rosemary Carter and her latest romance A WIFE AND CHILD. Next in the series is Barbara McMahon's DADDY AND DAUGHTERS. We'll be bringing you one deliciously cute **DADDY BOOM** title every month.

Who says bachelors and babies don't mix?

A WIFE
AND CHILD

BY
ROSEMARY CARTER

MILLS & BOON®

First published in Great Britain 1999
Harlequin Mills & Boon Limited,
Eton House, 18-24 Paradise Road, Richmond, Surrey TW9 1SR

© Rosemary Carter 1999

ISBN 0 263 81558 7

Set in Times Roman 10¼ on 10¾ pt.
02-9904-53267 C1

Printed and bound in Norway
by AIT Trondheim AS, Trondheim

CHAPTER ONE

"No!" The word shot explosively from the waitress's lips.

"Aw, let a man have a bit of fun."

Loathing in her expression, the young woman faced down the man with the tattooed arms and clothing damp with sweat. "No!" she exclaimed again.

Sterling Tayler, watching the scene from a nearby table, sensed that she was under great strain. For a moment, he wondered whether she meant to tip the contents of her tray—coffee, a dish piled high with bacon, eggs and French fries—into the man's lap. He found himself tensing.

But the waitress drew breath visibly, gripped the tray more tightly and took a step backward.

Unlike Sterling, the tattooed man seemed not to understand how close he had come to walking out of the diner with his clothes spattered with food and his dignity—if he had any—destroyed.

"Aw c'mon," he wheedled, reaching out to give an enticingly shaped bottom another pat. "I don't mean no harm. Just want a bit of fun before I hit the road again."

In an instant, the waitress increased the distance between them. "Not with me," she said angrily.

Her expression was furious, but her eyes had an odd haunted look. It wasn't the first time Sterling had noticed that look, just as it wasn't the first time he had seen her fending off unwelcome passes.

"Twelve hours I been driving my truck. Have to get a load of stuff to Sacramento before five. So why don't you give old Johnny a bit of a feel and a kiss? I'll be outta here after that."

5

"Don't touch me again!" the waitress warned. "You'll be sorry if you do, I promise you that."

Sara—he had heard the other waitresses call her that—was restraining herself, Sterling thought, and wondered whether her words were more than an idle threat. His food grew cold as he sat and watched the scene that was unfolding so close to him.

Sara fascinated him, so much so that he had come to the diner three days in a row. On his first visit to the small California town just outside San Francisco, his car had been parked nearby, and all he'd wanted was a quick cup of coffee before heading to his Napa Valley wine estate. For a man who didn't particularly enjoy going to diners, three consecutive visits was a lot—especially when well over an hour's drive each way was involved.

It was Sara who had drawn him back time after time. At first, he had merely been captivated by a sweet face and a pretty figure. Three days later, intrigued by sad eyes and a haunted expression, he longed to get to know her better.

Her face was a perfect oval above a neck that looked almost too slender to hold up her head, and her lips were soft and turned up at the corners. But her eyes were her most striking feature. Gray, with just a hint of blue, they were large and sloe-shaped. Sterling longed to see Sara smile, yet until now he had seen only sadness and that odd haunted expression.

It was more than Sara's appearance that drew Sterling to the diner day after day. She had a fragility that caught at something deep inside him, an emotion he hadn't known he possessed. Her vulnerability touched him. Though she tried very hard to come across as assertive and confident—just look how she had stood up to the truck driver—Sterling sensed that her confidence was partly an act.

Paula, another waitress, drew Sara aside. Sterling was just close enough to hear her say, "You've barely been here two weeks, hon. When you've worked here longer, you'll understand that men like Johnny don't really mean bad."

"I *hate* to be touched," Sara said fiercely.

"Hey, girls, I'm waiting for my food," the tattooed man shouted.

"Coming right up, Johnny," Paula called. And in an undertone to Sara, "You still have his tray."

"Oh, God…I hadn't realized."

"He's not all that bad."

"He's a bum, Paula. And he has no right to paw me."

Paula shook her head, tossing long earrings against her neck. "Telling a guy like Johnny about rights, hon, is like throwing stones in a quarry. Goes in one ear and comes right out the other."

Sterling grinned at the irreverent mixing of metaphors, but Sara was not amused. "I can't stand it, Paula. No man, *no man* is allowed to touch me."

"Sure, Sara, I hear you." Paula's tone was placating. "Give me Johnny's tray, I'll give him his food."

Gray eyes lit with relief. "Would you really?"

"Sure, why not? I can handle myself, the odd straying hand doesn't bother me. And don't worry about the tip. You can have it—if he gives one. The boss is watching, Sara, so just hand me the tray."

But Sara reconsidered. "I'll do it, Paula. It's my job, and I can't let that guy get the better of me. Thanks all the same."

A watching Sterling felt like standing up and applauding. Clearly, Sara was not about to let a boorish man intimidate her. The look of almost transparent delicacy notwithstanding, she was evidently strong-willed and determined.

That, too, was something he had glimpsed in her previously. It was potent, that odd mixture of vulnerability and assertiveness. The young woman was a mystery. Sterling couldn't keep his eyes off her.

She put the tray on Johnny's table, then stepped away quickly and deliberately.

Coffeepot in hand, she came to Sterling. "Would you care for a refill, sir?"

Her voice was low and clear, a very beautiful voice, Sterling thought. He longed to engage her in conversation, to hear her laugh. Even the way she phrased the question was different from the other waitresses, whose form of address was usually, "More coffee, hon?" Sara's classiness was peculiarly out of place in the diner.

"Thank you," Sterling said. "I'd appreciate another cup."

For some reason, she looked straight at him. Her gaze was unexpectedly questioning, as if something he'd said had surprised her. But the look didn't last more than a few seconds. A moment later she was pouring his coffee.

"You don't have to let him get away with it, you know," Sterling said quietly, nodding his head in Johnny's direction.

Once more she looked at him. "Seems to go with the territory." Her voice was suddenly flat.

"It shouldn't."

"No." Clearly, she had no wish to go on talking.

As she walked away, Sterling began to sip his coffee. There were a number of things he still needed to do that day, and yet he lingered.

His thoughts were with his work when there was another shouted exclamation. *"How dare you!"*

Lifting his head, Sterling was just in time to see Sara pulling away violently from a pair of grubby fingers that were pinching her bottom through her black miniskirt.

"I warned you not to do that!" She was furious.

"Cool it, hon," Paula advised quietly.

"That's right, cool it, girl." An unrepentant Johnny laughed too loudly. "Relax, sweetie, have some fun."

Sterling thought he would choke with anger as the man lunged at Sara. She saw him coming and jerked backward. As she did so, she bumped into the huge bulk of her boss, commonly known as Big Bill, who was advancing on the scene. The collision jolted Sara's right arm. Johnny let out an outraged roar as hot coffee splashed his clothes.

"Bitch!" he bellowed. "Damned bitch! She burned me, Big Bill!"

"Not on purpose." Sara was shaking. "It was an accident. You bumped into me, Big Bill."

"What the hell are you talking about? And what's the matter with you, anyway?" her boss ranted. "Why aren't you more careful? Clumsy broad! I've yet to see you carry more than two plates at a time. And talk about slow? Now this." He turned to Johnny. "You okay, fella?"

"Do I look okay?" the tattooed man countered belligerently. "My clothes are a mess, and it's days before I get home for fresh ones. What are you going to do about it, Big Bill?" The man wore an injured expression as he looked at a shirt that had been filthy even before the mishap. "That's what I want to know, Big Bill—how you going to put things right?"

The owner of the diner shot Sara a vicious look before turning to his unhappy customer. "Don't get yourself all steamed, Johnny. I'll give you money for a dry-clean."

"From the girl's wages, I hope," the man said vengefully.

"Well, sure—what else? You don't think I'm going to fork out the money from the till?"

"My wages?" Sara's small face paled.

"You heard, girl." Big Bill turned to Johnny. "What's that you been eating? Bacon, eggs and French fries? Sara here will get you another helping. On the house this time, fella."

"Jump to it," Johnny ordered Sara. He looked only slightly mollified.

In Sterling, a murderous rage was beginning to build. At thirty-four, he couldn't remember the last time he'd felt so protective toward a woman, but he felt that way now. Taking in the scene, the fragile girl, the two uncouth men, the gum-chewing waitresses watching from the sides, he was seized with a longing to carry Sara out of the diner, away from embarrassment and humiliation. It was only through sheer force of will that he kept himself from landing punches on the jaws of both men.

"I'll get the order," Paula said quietly to Sara.

"Nothin' doin'," came Johnny's quick rejoinder. "She'll get it. *Sara.*"

And Big Bill said, "Why you still standing there, girl?"

Pleadingly, Sara looked at her red-faced employer. "Big Bill..." she began.

"You heard him," Johnny said viciously. And then, to Sterling's disbelief, he reached out and pinched Sara again.

Until that moment, Sterling had somehow managed to control his temper, but this was too much! He was on his feet in an instant. All thoughts of restraint forgotten, he descended on the scene. Seizing the truck driver's grubby hand, he yanked it away from Sara, pulling it hard behind Johnny's neck.

"Leave the lady alone," Sterling snarled.

With an exclamation of pain, Johnny lifted his free hand in readiness for a punch. Big Bill pulled him back.

"Now, Johnny, I don't allow no fighting. Rules of the establishment. You know that."

"Tell this guy your rules," Johnny protested angrily. And to Sterling, "Want to settle something, man? I'll be happy to oblige."

Once more Big Bill held Johnny back. To Sterling he said, "Keep out of this, will you?" And to Johnny, "Cool it, fella, you don't want to tangle with the guy."

Ignoring the warning, Johnny shouted roughly, "Gonna go outside and fight, man?"

"I don't care to fight, and not because I couldn't beat you," Sterling said coldly. He threw Big Bill a hard look. "The lady was being harassed."

"The so-called lady is a waitress, and I'm taking care of things." The owner of the diner was clearly resentful.

"I've watched you take care, as you call it, and I didn't like what I saw."

"You don't understand the half of it."

"I understand very well, Bill. This man here has never learned how to take no for an answer. It's time he did."

"Now see here," a furious Johnny began, still straining to get away from Big Bill.

At that moment, a white-faced Sara said quietly to Sterling, "Please...don't make trouble for me."

Trouble? He threw her an uncomprehending look. What on earth was the woman talking about? Didn't she understand that he was only trying to help her?

"Girl's been a problem since she started here," Big Bill said. "No good as a waitress. Too many problems with the customers. Takes friendliness a darn sight too seriously."

"Problems you won't have to concern yourself with any longer. How much do you owe her?" Sterling's tone was curt.

"What?" Big Bill stared at him, eyes narrowed in their folds of red flesh.

"You heard me the first time. Wages. Back pay. How much do you owe her?"

"Don't do this!" Sara cried desperately, but Sterling didn't hear her.

"You're saying she's quitting?" Big Bill stared speculatively at Sterling.

"As of this minute."

"No!" Sara pleaded. "Big Bill, don't listen to him. Please! I don't know this man, he has no right to end my job for me. Big Bill—"

She put her hand on her employer's arm, but he shrugged it off easily. "Wages, less the cost of cleaning Johnny's clothes," he told Sterling.

"No," Sara said. She was shaking so violently that she had to hold on to the nearest table for support.

"Sara has no obligation to pay this man's cleaning bill," Sterling said quietly. "It's not her fault she was molested."

"Want to go to court on it?"

"If need be." Sterling's tone was disdainful. Beside him, he heard Sara gasp.

"Okay with me, too," Big Bill said.

"Of course," Sterling went on, "I can't promise to keep the case out of the press. There's a lot of interest these days in harassment in the workplace. I wouldn't be answerable if your business suffered as a result. How much is a cleaning bill for a shirt? Not more than a few bucks. Seems like a small amount when you think of all that negative publicity."

Big Bill looked as if he was about to burst a few blood vessels, but he knew when he was beaten. "Forget the deduction," he said bitterly, then named a figure. "Just get the girl out of here, and I'd appreciate it if you don't come back here again, either."

Once more, Sara touched her employer's arm. "This is crazy! Nobody asked me what *I* think. You men can't just go deciding things over my head as if I didn't exist. I'm not going anywhere. I'm not leaving the diner. This is my job, Big Bill."

"*Was* your job," he told her nastily. "This man here did me one hell of a favor when he quit for you."

"But he didn't! He can't." Sara shot Sterling an unhappy look. "Tell him."

The despairing eyes shafted their way into a spot deep inside Sterling's heart. But he had no intention of giving in to Sara's pleading. Decisively, he said, "I'm taking you out of this place. Now."

"You hear him, girl." Big Bill shoved a wad of bills into her hand. "Get out of here." And then, as he remembered something, "Get out of your room, as well. You have two hours to vacate."

Room? Sterling had no idea what the man was talking about. All he knew was that he had to take Sara out of this insufferable place.

"Come," he said.

She stepped away from him quickly. Thinking she might plead with Big Bill again, or worse still, apologize to Johnny—ideas that were to Sterling intolerable—he took her hand.

In a second, something tightened inside him. Sara's hand was so small, so delicate. As if it might break if he held it too tightly.

The impression lasted no more than a few seconds. By then, she had pulled her hand out of his.

"You're no better than those others," she hissed, when they emerged from the diner and into the street. "All you want is to touch. Nobody—*nobody* touches me without my permission."

Sterling looked at her, confused by her words. She was like a small wounded animal, he thought, trapped, cornered, yet determined to put up a fight.

"I haven't touched you, Sara."

"My hand." The haunted expression that seemed so much a part of her was stronger than ever.

"I just wanted to get you out of the place," he said. "Surely you're not comparing me with Johnny?"

"I know about men." There was an inexplicable fierceness in Sara's tone.

"Do you?" Sterling demanded. "In that case, I'd think you'd know when a man has bad intentions—and when he hasn't."

"All I know is, I don't want men touching me," she said stubbornly.

There was something he did not understand. Reasonably, he said, "I was just trying to help."

"And that's another thing! You had no right to lose my job for me!"

Sterling shot her a look of disbelief. "Are you telling me that after what happened you'd have gone on working in the diner? Your working conditions were appalling."

"I was dealing with them."

"Unsuccessfully."

"In your eyes, perhaps. But I was dealing with them. It's true, I hated having a man like Johnny paw me. So humiliating… But at least he wasn't actually hurting me."

God, but she was a contradictory and ungrateful female! "You heard what Big Bill said—he was going to fire you anyway."

"I'd have found a way of getting him to let me stay on." Traffic swirled about them as Sara looked up at Sterling—a long way up, it seemed to him. "Big Bill was right about one thing, you know—I'm not the greatest waitress. The other women are all much more efficient than I am. But I'd have learned, in time. Now, thanks to you, I don't have the chance."

Sterling was silent as he tried to absorb what she'd said. "How about Johnny?" he asked at last.

Sara's lips tightened. "If he had come again, one of the others would have traded tables with me. Some of them take passes in their stride. I'm not saying they like them, but they don't seem to loathe them as much as I do. The point is, I'd have worked something out."

Sterling shook his head. "I don't understand—a woman like you, why would you make an effort to stay in a place like that?"

"It was a job. A job I no longer have—thanks to you."

"A job you needed that badly?"

"That badly." Her tone was bitter.

People passed them on the sidewalk, but Sterling didn't notice them. Restlessly, he shoved his hands into the pockets of his pants. "I'm sure you'll find something else."

"I appreciate your confidence," she said sarcastically.

Never in his life had Sterling felt so defensive with a woman. He hated feeling this way. Especially with this woman.

"Look," he said slowly, "perhaps I can help."

The look she shot him was unfriendly. "You've done quite enough already."

"You don't know that, Sara. There could be a way."

"I'm quite sure there isn't. Anyway, I have to go now."

It was Sterling's cue to go, too. And yet he couldn't just walk away. "What will you do, Sara?"

"Whatever it is, it doesn't concern you."

"I'm sure you really will find something." He tried to sound convincing.

"In any event," she said, "you don't need to worry about me."

"Sara..."

"Goodbye."

"Not so fast."

"I have things to do." Her shoulders were straight, her head held high.

Inside the pockets of his pants, Sterling's hands clenched. This slight, angry woman was really getting to him, and he didn't like the feeling at all. He found himself saying, "I want you to understand—I did what I had to. I did it for you."

"I believe you really think that." Her expression was tight. "Now I do have to go."

She was walking away when Sterling called her name, and she turned. "Yes?"

"I know I keep saying it, but I'm sure you really will be okay."

Sara gave a small, hard laugh. "Without you interfering in my life, I just might be."

Nothing much a man could reply to a put-down like that. So Sterling said, "Fine, perhaps I'll see you around some time," and walked away without another word.

His intentions had been good, he told himself, as he made his way to his car. When he had removed Sara from a bad situation, he hadn't expected her to be quite so upset. Such was the thanks he had received for his efforts. Not that he had expected thanks.

And he had tried to offer his help afterward, an offer she had refused. That was what he must remember. Sara had made it clear she could take care of herself. Fragile she might be, but she was also prickly and assertive. She would be okay, just as she said.

If only he could forget that haunted look.

His car was parked halfway down the block. Abruptly,

he got in and swung into the road. He couldn't have said why he glanced into his rearview mirror.

Sara was walking down the street away from him. There was an unconscious swing to her walk, a movement of hips and the pretty little bottom Johnny had found so entrancing. As did Sterling, though he would not have dreamed of showing his feelings so crudely.

It was a moment before he saw past the pretty figure to the droop of Sara's shoulders. Face to face, she had been one spirited female. Now that she thought herself unobserved, she was the picture of dejection.

Sterling watched her a few seconds longer, and once more the vulnerability and despair of the slender, feisty little female struck a chord deep inside him. His anger vanished as he pulled the car alongside the curb. Seconds later he was running after Sara.

She spun around as he called her name. "You!" she exclaimed, jerking away from him as he touched her arm.

"Me," he said quietly, and forced himself to ignore a feeling of rejection.

"I thought you'd gone."

"I came back. We need to talk."

As she shook her head, her hair moved on her shoulders, and Sterling noticed the golden lights that gilded fair curls. Involuntarily, he lifted his hand, driven by the compulsion to run his fingers through her hair. In the nick of time, he remembered Sara's aversion to being touched, and he dropped his hand. But the longing remained.

"Talk?" Sara eyed him wearily. "I thought we'd done all our talking."

"There are two restaurants farther down the road."

"We can talk here."

"On a street corner? I don't think so, Sara."

"I don't have time to waste. Besides, I don't date men."

For the first time he noticed dark rings beneath the sloe-shaped eyes. If only he could wrap his arms around her and never let her go.

Pleasantly, he said, ''This isn't a date.''

''As long as you understand that.''

''But we do need a place to sit.''

She looked as if she needed a decent meal, as if she hadn't eaten in far too long, but Sterling sensed that she would scurry away if he said so.

''There's a steak house. There's also a place that specializes in Chinese food. Take your pick, Sara.''

''I'm not at all hungry, and I don't feel like eating.''

''I asked you to choose.''

Perhaps Sara was swayed by the won't-take-no-for-an-answer tone in Sterling's voice. She hesitated a moment before her lips lifted in the slightest hint of a smile.

''Chinese,'' she said, ''and only because I'm less likely to find a job there than at the steak house.''

If the tiny smile was enchanting, she would be breath-takingly beautiful if she let herself smile properly.

''Let's go,'' Sterling said, and was careful to keep his distance from Sara as they crossed the road.

They were lucky enough to find a quiet table in a corner of the restaurant. Sara said again that she wasn't hungry, but Sterling insisted on ordering for them both anyway. The lemon-fried chicken was reputed to be good, as was the shrimp chow mein.

When the waiter had left the table, he sat back in his chair. It was really quite extraordinary how much he enjoyed looking at Sara. This was what had drawn him to the diner when he had more important things to do, her lovely gray eyes and delicate features, the otherworldly transparency of her face. Even when Sara was angry—as she undoubtedly was now—there was a sweetness in her expression. He wondered how it would feel to kiss her. Sheer bliss, he decided.

''You're not at all sorry, are you?'' she asked accusingly.

Sorry that the lustful Johnny would never again touch her? That Big Bill would never again address her with disrespect?

"No," Sterling said, "I'm not sorry you left the diner."

"Well, why would you be? You had your moment of masculine glory. It must have given you enormous satisfaction."

Grimly, Sterling said, "Is that what you think it was all about? Some aggressive macho act?"

"Wasn't it?" She tossed the question at him.

"I did what I had to, I keep telling you that."

"What *you* assumed you had to."

"Contrary to what you might think, Sara," he said tightly, "I don't get my kicks out of intimidating lechers."

"I see." Her tone indicated that she didn't see at all.

"Look," he said after a moment, quietly, "I'm sorry you have a problem. I really am sorry about that."

"An enormous problem." She glanced at her watch. "And I don't have time to lose. You heard Big Bill, I have to be out of the room in two hours. Less than two hours, with all the time I've wasted."

"I don't understand about the room," Sterling said.

"It's above the diner."

"Are all the waitresses provided with accommodation?"

"Only one. Me, in this case. When I started at the diner, someone else had just left. I was given the room at a reduced rent. I had to do certain extra chores in return."

Sterling was beginning to understand Sara's despair. "So now you have to find a place to live."

"That first. Then a job. Salary with which to pay my rent."

Not for the first time, Sterling told her he was certain she would find something, but even as he said the words, he was aware of how hollow and inadequate they sounded.

Obviously, Sara thought so, too, for she turned on him furiously. "You speak with all the smugness of a person who has never had to worry about food or shelter."

His heart went out to her. "Things are really that bad?"

The lovely eyes met his for a long moment. Then she turned away, but not before he saw the glimmer of tears.

Inside Sterling, something wrenched. "Tell me about it," he invited quietly.

"I..." Just for a second Sara looked tempted. Then the shutters came down over her eyes. "No."

"Please." Reaching across the table, he folded his big hands over her small ones. "Please, Sara," he said urgently.

Her fingers quivered beneath his. When Sara drew her hands away, Sterling did not try to stop her.

Her cheeks were flushed as she glanced once more at her watch. "I don't know why I'm sitting here. I have to go."

"Not before you've eaten."

"I told you I wasn't hungry."

"I'd like you to eat anyway. I think I see the waiter loading up our food."

"But—"

"You wouldn't walk out on me now, surely?"

The blatant appeal to Sara's conscience had her biting her lower lip. Briefly, Sterling felt ashamed of the tactic, but the moment passed. He wanted to see Sara eat. He also knew that he wanted to prolong the sheer pleasure of her presence at the table—even if she didn't seem to be enjoying his company one bit.

"This is a mistake," she said unhappily.

"It isn't. When we've finished, I'll help you move your things from your room."

She seemed to withdraw into herself at the words. "I don't allow men into my room."

"I'm not going to hurt you, Sara."

He was startled when Sara flinched quite violently. For a moment, she looked so pale that Sterling wondered if she was going to faint. Then, so softly that he had to strain to hear her, Sara said, "No men in my room. That's just the way it is."

"Sara—"

"I appreciate your concern, but I don't need it. I wish you'd accept that."

Sterling couldn't accept it, but he knew better than to tell her so. "Where will you go?"

"I don't know. Not yet. But I'll find a place before nightfall. I have to." She tried to sound convincing, but Sterling saw the fear that she could not dispel from her eyes as she spoke.

They were silent as the food was put before them—at just the right moment, as far as Sterling was concerned. When they had finished eating, they would take their leave of each other, and that would be that. Sara had made it clear she didn't want his help, and in the circumstances he might as well shed the sense of responsibility that had been weighing heavily on him since leaving the diner.

A little angrily, he plunged his fork into a piece of golden lemon chicken. All at once, he couldn't wait for the meal to end. Sara, he noticed, was not eating at all.

"Don't fancy the food?" he asked lightly.

"It's great." And then, on an afterthought, "Thank you."

In spite of himself, Sterling grinned. "You don't know it's great. You haven't touched it."

She was even paler than before. "I did tell you I wasn't hungry."

When, Sterling wondered, would she have her next meal? "Can't you manage a little? Humor me, Sara."

"I'll try."

Sara picked up her fork and speared a piece of chicken, only to put it down again. She pushed a few bean sprouts from one side of the plate to the other. She was playing with the food, Sterling saw. And then, perhaps because she felt his eyes on her, she lifted a piece of chicken to her lips. The action seemed to involve conscious effort.

A moment later, she said, "Excuse me." And then she was on her feet and running from the table in the direction of the washrooms. Astonished, Sterling watched her go.

He was wondering whether to follow her—he could ask some woman to look for Sara even if he could not enter the ladies' washroom himself—when she returned.

Sitting down, she said in a low voice, "I'm so sorry."

Sterling leaned toward her. "You're not well."

"I'm fine, really, I am."

Sterling could see she was making an effort not to cry. Her face was ashen, and her eyes, those gorgeous eyes, seemed drained of all color.

Sterling felt a tearing pain deep inside him, a great swell of compassion. "I'm not blind, Sara. I can see you're not fine at all."

"I wish I could make you believe me. I... I had a bad moment. Something I ate...maybe yesterday. But I'm fine now."

As if to prove it, she picked up her fork once more. But that was as far as she got.

Helplessly, she looked at Sterling. "I can't... I'm sorry you wasted your money buying me a meal."

"Don't give it a thought. No point in eating if you don't feel up to it."

"No." She put the fork down.

"Let's think about the next step, Sara."

"There is no next step for you."

But there was, Sterling knew that. The temporary relief he had felt at being absolved of responsibility for Sara had been replaced by a deep concern.

"You need a job."

"That's right."

"Does it have to be a restaurant?"

She hesitated before saying, "Yes, I think so."

"You haven't always been a waitress, Sara."

She looked at him tensely without answering.

"In fact, I'd say the diner was your first time waiting tables. What did you do before that?"

"No questions, please."

"Why not? Have you worked before, Sara?"

She nodded.

Well, a nod was better than nothing. Encouraged, he said, "Are you going to tell me what you did?" And when she remained silent, ''I thought women loved to talk about their careers.''

''I don't.'' Her voice was brittle.

At least she wasn't walking out on him. Sterling decided to persist. ''I only ask because you might be able to find something in the same line of work.''

''No,'' she said, and went on after a moment. ''I may not be a good waitress yet—I know I'm not—but I'll learn. I have to.'' She stood up. ''And now I really do have to go.''

''Wait,'' Sterling said, as she started to walk from the table. ''Does the job have to be here—in this town?'' The question left his lips almost at the moment the thought entered his mind.

She shrugged. ''I've no ties here.''

''How about a job on a wine estate?''

Hope touched her face, warming her eyes and bringing some color to her face. ''A wine estate? What would I do there?''

''Fill in for the secretary who's on a two-month leave of absence.''

Relief joined the hope in her expression. ''Secretarial work?''

''Correspondence. Some bookkeeping.'' He was watching her closely. ''Nothing very complicated. Nothing you couldn't learn on the job. Perhaps you've done some secretarial work in the past?''

''Yes,'' she said, ''I have.''

In which case, Sterling wondered, why was she looking for a job in a restaurant, a line of work for which she was obviously unsuited and unqualified?

''A job like that could be the answer,'' Sara said.

''For the owner, too. The person who was to take on the job found something else at the last moment.''

Her eyes moved from his. ''Would I...need references?''

''Not for a temporary job like this.''

''Two months, you said?'' Her gaze met his once more.

"About that."

He had her full attention. The eyes searching his shone with eagerness and intelligence.

"Interested, Sara?"

"Maybe." And then, "Where is this wine estate?"

"In the Napa Valley."

"Far from here?"

"About an hour."

"A lonely place."

"You could call it that."

His answer didn't appear to put her off. If anything, it seemed to please her.

"The owners. You don't know they'll want me."

"I do know." Sterling smiled at her. "I am the owner, Sara."

Her expression changed as she stared at him. A veil seemed to descend over her eyes, and suddenly the tension was back in her face.

"You?"

"Is that a problem?"

"I know nothing about you. Not even your name."

"I hadn't realized!" He was startled. He hadn't thought of introducing himself, perhaps because he felt as if he'd known her always. "All this time I've been calling you Sara, and it never occurred to me that you didn't know my name. I'm Sterling Tayler."

"Sterling Tayler," she said slowly. "There are things I'll need to know, Mr. Tayler."

"Such as?"

If Sterling had expected her to be overcome with gratitude, he had been mistaken. Sara's wariness was beginning to annoy him.

"Are you married?" she asked.

"Lord, no!"

"Oh." She looked dismayed.

"That's a problem, Sara?"

His unmarried state had never been an obstacle before.

If anything, it had made him a target of attention from many single women and not a few married ones.

Sara hesitated. Then she asked cautiously, "Who else is at the estate, Mr. Tayler?"

"Men who work in the fields and in the wineries. And please call me Sterling."

"Any women?"

"Some of the men are married."

"Where do they live?"

She really was the most peculiar girl. "There are staff quarters. Speak any Spanish, Sara?"

The question seemed to surprise her. "No."

"Most of the people on the estate are from Mexico. Some of them don't speak English. If you don't speak their language, you won't be able to converse with them."

Sara looked unhappy. "I don't think I can take the job."

Sterling's shrug hid an odd disappointment. "It has to be your decision."

"It isn't personal…"

"Really?" His voice was hard.

"You see, I won't be alone with a man. *Any* man. You have to understand that."

There it was again, the mixture of defiance and despair in her eyes and in her voice. Sterling did not allow himself to be moved by it. "I don't understand," he said briefly, "though I might if you explained."

A closed look appeared in Sara's face. "I can't. Thanks for the offer, but I'll have to make other plans."

Sterling pushed his plate aside. "That's it, then. You're not eating a thing, Sara, and I seem to have lost my appetite. I thought I could help you out with a job, but obviously I can't. In the meanwhile, I'm holding you up. Keeping you here when you have things to do. You don't have to wait while I settle the bill."

"Thank you." She pushed back her chair. "You must think I'm ungrateful. I still wish you hadn't quit my job for me, but I realize you were trying to help."

"Skip the thanks, I don't want them." Sterling made no effort to conceal his impatience.

"Yes, well… Goodbye."

He tried not to watch her as she walked out of the restaurant. He caught the waiter's eye, asked for the bill and declined an offer to bag the uneaten food.

Minutes later, he heard Sara's voice. "Mr. Tayler…"

He had been filling out the credit slip and hadn't seen her return. He decided not to show his surprise as he looked up. "Yes?"

"I've been thinking…."

Sterling was impatient enough not to make it easy for her, even though he could sense, from the look in her eyes, what was coming. At this point, Sara would have to spell things out.

"I may want to change my mind—if the offer's still open."

"My marital status hasn't changed in the last two minutes."

"I know that."

"And the estate is still not populated with women who speak your language and will be your friends."

"Forget I asked," she said, and turned on her heel.

It was Sterling's turn to relent. "Sara…"

She looked at him. The face that had been ashen such a short time ago was flushed with anger. "Forget it, I said. I didn't get out of one intolerable situation just to land myself in another."

She was utterly gorgeous when she was angry, Sterling thought. "Now listen—"

"Please…forget it."

"What will you do?"

"I'll figure something out."

"Sara—"

"Thanks for the meal, Mr. Tayler. It's not your fault I didn't eat."

She walked quickly to the door of the restaurant and into the street. Sterling had a rancid taste on his tongue.

He did not climb down easily, but he knew that if he let Sara walk out of his life, he would regret it. There were times when a man had to bend.

He caught up with her as she was about to cross the road. "Sara…"

She looked at him. "What now?"

"If you still want the job, it's yours. In fact, I would be very glad if you accepted it."

She didn't snatch at the offer as he'd thought—hoped—she would.

"You were playing a game with me back at the restaurant."

"I was," he admitted. "Do you want the job?"

There was a yearning in her eyes, but her voice remained firm. "As long as one thing is clear. I won't tolerate any liberties. No passes, Mr. Tayler."

Sterling wondered if the time would come when he would understand her. "I think you've made that clear by now."

"Not from you. Not from anybody else, either."

This had to be the strangest job interview Sterling had ever conducted. A fire truck raced past, sirens blaring, making conversation impossible for at least half a minute.

When she could be heard, Sara said, "That's a condition."

"Unnecessary, but okay with me. When would you like to start?"

"I'm available any time, you know that," she said quietly. Even in the face of a problem she did not want to discuss, Sara retained her dignity.

"Today then—if it suits you?"

Some of the tension drained from the slender figure. "It does suit me." She looked at her watch. "I need to get my things from my room. If you'll tell me where to meet you?"

"I'll come with you."

"I don't think that's a good idea."

"Sure it is," he told her, in a voice that did not allow

for debate. "We'll park my car by the diner and load up. At least, we'll take as much as we can get in. Perhaps your charming ex-employer won't mind storing the rest until we can make a second trip."

"A second trip won't be necessary. There isn't very much," she said faintly.

"One thing, Sara." He didn't touch her, though he longed to. "I want you to know, I'm not Johnny or Big Bill. You're not going into a situation like the diner. You may even enjoy living on a wine estate."

"Oh, I hope so."

For the first time, Sara smiled at him, a real smile this time, with lips curving enticingly upwards and gray eyes warm and sparkling. The effect was electrifying. Sterling felt his heart turn an unexpected somersault.

He swallowed hard, but he knew better than to let her see how deeply she affected him. "Let's go then," was all he said.

CHAPTER TWO

SARA was tight with nerves as Sterling followed her to the room above the diner. Not since the day she'd fled from Larry had she been alone with a man. And in such a tiny space. So confined. Out of earshot of all but the loudest screams. Who knew, even if she was heard, whether anyone would come to her aid?

As Sara stopped outside the door, a shivering began deep inside her. "Wait here." She tried very hard to conceal her fear.

Sterling looked at her from his great height—the man had to be six foot four if he was an inch! When he spoke, his voice was deep and vital and as overwhelmingly masculine as everything else about him.

"I'm going to help you carry your stuff," he said.

"I'll bring it all to the door. There isn't much. A couple of suitcases. And a few other odds and ends."

He lifted an eyebrow quizzically. "Quicker if we both put things together."

Didn't the man know how to take a hint? "As I said, there's not much."

"Even so." There was that edge in his tone she'd heard in the restaurant once or twice.

"I prefer it that way, Mr. Tayler."

"The name is Sterling. I'm in a hurry, Sara. I should have been back home long ago."

"I didn't ask you to take me to lunch," she said defiantly.

"That's right." Unexpectedly, Sterling laughed.

The sound, so close to her, made Sara shiver. A different kind of shiver this time. Amazingly, it had nothing to do with fear.

28

"Nor," said that vital voice, "did you ask me to quit your job for you. But there's no point going into all that again. Are you going to let me into the room, Sara?" She still hesitated. "Or is there something you don't want me to know about? Some deep secret?" Dark eyes sparkled.

Actually, she had two secrets, and she didn't want him to know about either of them.

"Nothing that would concern you," she said faintly.

"There you go, then, you can let me help you." Sterling paused. "It's quite safe, Sara. I meant what I said, I'm not going to harm you."

Larry could have said the same thing, though not perhaps in quite the same way. Larry had his own particular brand of charm, a smooth, suave, polished kind of charm that lulled and persuaded and flattered and ultimately seduced. Sara had not recognized the danger of that charm until it was too late, and now she was paying the price for it.

Sterling was different from Larry, she admitted. Older, for one thing. Early thirties, she estimated. He was tough and unpretentious, with an air of intense physical strength. Nothing suave or polished about him.

Yet when you came down to it, there were only two things that mattered to men. Power and sex. Wiser now than she had been, Sara knew she would never again allow a man to take advantage of her.

"Your deadline is approaching," he reminded her. "I wouldn't put it past your sweet ex-boss to storm up here and chuck your things into the street."

He was right, of course. Big Bill would have no qualms about barging into the room and ruthlessly throwing out her possessions.

"I wasn't thinking about the deadline...."

Sterling's eyebrows lifted. "Meaning you're more frightened of me than of Big Bill? If that's so, it doesn't bode well for our working relationship."

In an odd way Sara did not care to acknowledge to herself, she really did fear Sterling more than her obnoxious ex-employer. At the same time, she needed, quite desperately, shelter and a salary, which made Sterling her only hope right now.

She met his gaze directly. "I'm not frightened."

"Glad to hear it."

"I may not appear very strong, but I'd fight any man who tried to hurt me."

Once more his eyebrows lifted. "Did I say something to provoke that?"

"I just need to make things clear at the start."

For a long moment Sterling looked at her, his eyes deep and dark and enigmatic. "I like a woman who knows how to stand up for herself."

And with that Sara had to be content. At least Sterling knew she was a woman to be reckoned with. While she could not match him for strength or size, even a small woman could defend herself with a well-aimed kick. She had learned that too late.

Sterling was silent as he followed her into the room. Sara hadn't realized quite how small it was until he was in it. It was as if Sterling's maleness dominated and filled every inch of space. The air was permeated with such raw sexuality that she wanted nothing more than to run as far and as fast as she could.

Had she exchanged one bad situation for another?

And to think that this man was now her employer. He was big in every way. Apart from his height, his shoulders were impossibly wide, and his chest, even under a sports shirt, had a strongly muscled look. Larry was possessed of a movie-style appearance, studied boyishness combined with a winsome smile. Sterling was handsome in an altogether different way. His eyes were dark and humorous, and his face was rugged, the skin tanned and weathered, as if he spent much of his time out-of-doors.

Under normal circumstances, Sara would probably have thought Sterling Tayler an extremely attractive man. But the circumstances were anything but normal.

"*This* is your home?" he asked, disbelief in his voice.

Sara tore her gaze from the tanned face and tried to look at the room, her temporary refuge, with Sterling's eyes. "It isn't home, exactly…"

"It doesn't look like a home at all."

In an instant she was angry. "It's all very well for you to be contemptuous, but—"

"I'm not contemptuous, Sara."

"Certainly sounds like it."

"I'm just trying to understand. There's nothing here."

"Not very much," she conceded.

"Less than that. It's clean and tidy, and…" He stopped, as if searching for a word. "Transitory," he said at last. "As if you arrived here in a hurry. And were ready to leave it just as quickly."

Sara felt the blood leaving her cheeks. "What are you trying to say? That I'm a woman on the run?"

"Are you?"

"Not from the law, if that's what you think," she said tersely.

The dark eyes studied her intently. "Then you are on the run."

"I didn't say that."

"You didn't have to. From what, Sara?" His tone was mild, but she sensed something inexorable behind the quietly asked question.

"Nothing that concerns you."

"Why won't you tell me?"

"I don't want to." Her voice crackled with tension.

"I see," he said slowly.

"You don't see at all. But no questions, Sterling. I can't have questions."

"It's natural for people to want to know certain things, Sara."

"In my case, it isn't possible." She faced him steadily. "Is that going to be a problem? Because if it is, it's best we both know it now. If you need the story of my life, there's no point in my working for you.''

Sterling took his time answering. Sara's throat was dry with nerves as she waited for him to speak. If he withdrew his offer, what would she do? Big Bill's deadline was fast approaching.

''It won't be a problem,'' Sterling said.

Sara exhaled sharply. ''Are you certain?''

He grinned at her, an easy grin, one that settled into the lines around his eyes and at the corners of his mouth. ''What man can resist a woman of mystery?''

''I really am not running from the law.''

''I believed you the first time. No need to say it again. Let's get going, Sara.''

It didn't take her long to pack her possessions—the clothes she had so hurriedly dumped into two suitcases in Maine, the photo of her parents, the locket-like pendant she had inherited from her grandmother. There was a chair she had picked up cheaply at a garage sale, for Big Bill had provided no more than a bed, a small table and an even smaller closet. There was also a print, bought at another sale, of a beach with children playing on the sands. The tranquil scene had made her long for a time when she had spent lazy mornings at the ocean with her family. A time that seemed to have existed in another world.

She was aware of Sterling's eyes on her while she packed, but she did not look at him.

''Ready,'' she said at last.

''Ten minutes from start to finish. Not many women who can do that.''

He picked up the chair and the suitcases, then made his way easily down the stairs. Sara followed, carrying the picture.

Big Bill was nowhere in sight as they passed the entrance to the restaurant, and Sara was glad of it. She was in no mood for another encounter with the man. But as they were walking toward Sterling's car, Paula came running after them.

"I was looking out for you, Sara. You okay?"

"I'm fine, thanks."

"Going out with him?" Eyes curious, Paula nodded in Sterling's direction.

"I'm going to work for him."

"You are?" The waitress looked amazed.

"He owns a wine estate in the Napa Valley."

"What kind of work, Sara?"

"His secretary's away, and I'm going to be filling in for her." Paula's expression was doubtful. Sara added, "A job, Paula, that's all it is."

"You can do office work?"

Sara hesitated before answering. "Yes."

Sterling had put the cases and the chair in the car. He looked at Sara as he opened the passenger door.

Paula threw her arms around Sara. "You take care, hon, do you hear? You can change your mind any time you want, you know that. Any problem, and you come back to town. You know where I live. I'll put you up, try to find you something else." At the last words, she glared at Sterling, as if warning him not to mistreat her friend.

A lump formed in Sara's throat at the other woman's kindness. "Thanks, Paula, thanks for everything."

"Hey, Paula!" Big Bill roared from inside the restaurant.

Paula rolled her eyes dramatically. "Bully," she muttered. The two women hugged again, and then Paula hurried to work and Sara got into the car.

Just minutes after leaving the outskirts of the town, Sara was beginning to regret not taking Paula up on her offer. Not since the trouble with Larry had she felt quite so disturbed—though in a different way. It was not that Sterling was doing anything he shouldn't. Not yet, anyway, though she'd defend herself if he did!

It was something in the air that bothered her. Sterling's presence in her room had been bad enough, the intensely masculine man dominating her space. In the car, the sexual tension filling the air was unbearable.

Sara sat as close to the window as she was able, but the seat was only so big, and Sterling was uncomfortably close to her. He was wearing navy pants, and the fabric clung to his legs, revealing length and tautness. Dark hair covered tanned arms bare to the elbow, arms that looked steel-hard and very strong. His hands, in particular, drew her eyes—though she tried not to look at them. Long hands, they were, well-shaped and cared for, but not manicured as Larry's had been. Sara sensed that Sterling's hands would be as hard as the rest of him—and as sexy.

The car sped around a bend in the road. Thrown off balance, Sara was unable to stop herself falling against Sterling. She jerked as his arm went around her shoulder.

"No!" she exclaimed. Nausea filled her throat—as well as a strange excitement.

The arm tightened just for a second, then left her shoulder. Sara exhaled, the breath scalding her throat.

"You shouldn't have." The words emerged shakily.

"Just helping you, Sara."

"Still..."

"If you thought that was a pass, you were mistaken," he said dryly.

Half a mile passed before Sara was able to say, "Okay."

For a long while they drove in silence, with Sara gazing out of the window at scenery that was quite different from the eastern seaboard. The houses looked much newer than the ones she was used to, the architecture often Spanish in style. Trucks passed the car loaded with artichokes and other vegetables. Wherever she looked there was a vibrancy that was quite different from the place where she had lived all of her twenty-four years.

Eventually, Sterling said, "Are you going to tell me what's wrong?"

"Wrong?" she asked, swinging to look at him.

"You must know your reactions are extreme."

He turned his head from the road, and for a long moment their eyes met and held, dark eyes holding her gray ones steadily. Wildly, Sara wondered how much Sterling saw in her expression, how much he could possibly guess.

"No questions," she reminded him.

"I can't help wondering."

"Maybe," she said shakily, "I should go back."

"You don't really mean that."

"I do."

"What would you do there?"

She thought of Paula and her offer of help. "I'd manage."

"No place to live, no job. You prefer the uncertainty of the town to the *dangers*—" the last word was spoken sarcastically "—of coming to work for me?"

"You just ask too many questions."

"I respect your right to privacy, but you seem very sensitive."

"Take me back to town!"

"You should have thought of that earlier," Sterling said curtly. "I'm already late getting home. The meal, and then going to your room, all took a lot longer than I expected. Now you want to turn back? No way, Sara."

"I didn't ask you to help me." Her voice was husky with distress.

Sterling glanced sideways once more, his expression hard to read. After a moment, he said, "Maybe I'm beginning to be sorry myself that I stepped in. Fact is, I did."

"You could still go back."

"I've wasted far too much time already. I offered you a job, and you accepted. That's just the way it is, Sara."

"I've changed my mind, Sterling."

"Tough," he said unsympathetically.

"You mean—" she tried not to show her fear "—that you'd hold me against my will at your estate?"

"Lord, Sara, I didn't take you for an irrational female." He sounded disgusted. "I'm not going to lock you up in some cage and throw away the key. But you will have to stay the night. In the morning, I can have one of the men drive you back to town.''

"Stop the car," she ordered.

With a screeching of brakes on the shoulder of the road, an irate Sterling did just that. "Want to walk back?" he demanded.

"If you won't drive me."

"I've already told you I won't."

"If you'll open the trunk, I'll get out my cases."

"Sure. One thing, though—any idea how far it is from here to town?"

"Not exactly."

"Forty miles, give or take a mile. Think you can cover the distance before dark?"

He was being sarcastic, of course, Sara thought. Forty miles! Incredible that they could have driven so far without her knowing it. She must have been even more pre-occupied with Sterling than she had realized.

She looked at him in disbelief. "That far?"

"You'd have to spend the night in a hotel somewhere."

She hadn't thought of that. Hotel accommodation would cost more than she could afford. Precious little would be left of the money Big Bill had paid her, and she needed every cent.

As if he read her thoughts, Sterling said, "Unless you intend hitching a ride."

"A ride," Sara echoed faintly.

"Lots of men will stop to pick up a pretty girl."

"I don't think—"

"Of course," he went on pleasantly, "you don't know what kind of guy will stop. Ten to one, he'll be honorable. On the other hand, he might not be. And whatever you may think of me, Sara, I'm not about to drag you behind some bush and assault you."

There was no way she would hitch a ride. She read all the time about women who went with strangers and were found beaten up or worse. She had already had enough trauma to last her a lifetime.

She did not look at Sterling as she said, "I'll go with you."

"If you're sure that's what you want." His tone was polite, but Sara knew he was amused.

She was relieved that Sterling didn't try to make small talk as he drove on. She was even more relieved when he turned on the radio and the sound of country music filled the air. The cheerful sound seemed to lessen the tension between them.

He had been driving about an hour when Sterling said, "We're in the Napa Valley now."

Sara gazed with interest through the car window. Despite her tension, she was struck by the beauty all around her. The rolling vineyards, the gracious homesteads, many of them offering bed-and-breakfast facilities, the distant hills and beyond those, mountains.

"Mountain View," Sterling said, the next time he spoke.

Sara turned to him. "Your estate?"

"That's right."

"Where?"

He lifted a hand from the wheel and gestured. "All the land hereabouts."

She looked in the direction he pointed. Acre upon acre of land stretching toward the hills. Rich-looking land, all of it covered with trellises and vines.

"It's beautiful!" The words escaped her lips involuntarily.

"You think so?" Sterling asked, and there was no mistaking the curiosity in his tone. "I know why I love the wine country, but I wonder what it can mean to you."

"It's so big," Sara said slowly. "So...so spacious. A person could be free here."

"Free?" Sterling prompted.

Still looking across the vineyards, Sara said, "Free to live any way you want. Free from other people, from pressures and pettiness. Free from having to do things you loathe.''

Sterling was quiet a long moment. At length, he said, ''Guess I never thought about it that way before now.''

''You never thought about it,'' Sara said fervently, ''because you don't know any other life.''

''And you do?'' he asked quietly.

She was about to say yes when a hand covered hers. A big hand, sun-warmed and strong. A shiver ran up Sara's wrist and all the way up her arm. For a long moment she sat quite still as the big male hand folded over hers.

And then she remembered who she was, where and with whom. In an instant, the shiver of excitement—*was it possible that she could still be excited by a man?*—turned to one of utter revulsion. Violently, she jerked her hand from his.

''How dare you!'' she exclaimed.

''I didn't mean anything, Sara.''

''I told you I won't be touched.''

''I'm sorry,'' he said. ''It was the way you talked.''

''What did I say?''

''Beauty and freedom. Something in your voice I hadn't heard before. Passion. Wonder.''

She had let down her guard, that was what had happened. The loveliness of the Napa Valley had got to her, unleashing emotions that had been buried for so long she had been unaware of their existence. For a few seconds she had forgotten her secrets. She hadn't thought of what the man beside her would make of her words. How could she have been so stupid?

Unhappily, Sara pulled herself closer to the edge of the seat. ''Forget I said any of it,'' she told Sterling.

''How can I? You intrigue me.'' His voice was low and vibrant.

''I'm really quite boring.'' Her voice was tinged with despair.

''I don't pretend to understand you, Sara, but you're not boring.''

"There's nothing to understand," she insisted.

"We both know better than that."

"Besides, by tomorrow I'll probably be gone, and it won't matter whether you understand me or not."

After a long moment, Sterling said, "Yes. Right."

They did not talk again until he turned the car off the road and drove between two wooden gates.

He turned to her. "Welcome to Mountain View. The house is farther down the road."

Despite her intention to leave the next day, Sara was unable to hide her interest as Sterling drove along a road bordered with oaks. Shrubs grew between the trees, and beyond them, Sara caught more glimpses of the vineyards.

As they rounded a bend, a house came into view, and Sara caught her breath at the sight of it. It was built in Spanish style, and its white walls were covered with creepers. Decorative wrought-iron work framed the windows. The roof was made of red tiles, and the sun caught it so that it looked as if it was on fire. An exquisite house, Sara thought.

Wham!

Sara gasped, her eyes jerking from the house as something bounced on the front window of the car, then rolled into the road. A ball, she saw. It was another moment before she saw the group of children at the roadside. One boy, taller than the others, lowered his arm.

The brakes gave a protesting screech as the car stopped abruptly. A second later, Sterling had flung open his door, leaped into the road and seized the ball.

Sara's every nerve tightened as she took in the scene— the powerful man, the children, the miscreant who had thrown the ball. She knew what would happen. Could picture, even before it occurred, the punishment Sterling would mete out. The boy with the outstretched arm would be beaten. Would the others pay for the accident, as well?

"*Señor!*" the tall boy shouted. He was a beautiful lad, his teeth very white in an olive skin, his dark eyes sparkling with life and laughter.

The animation would leave his face the moment Sterling's fist connected with his jaw. Sara, who knew only too well how such a blow would feel, was tight with nerves and nausea.

As Sterling advanced on the children, Sara knew she could not stand what was about to happen. She could not allow it. Without any thought for her safety, without pausing to consider what she was doing, knowing only that she had to protect the beautiful boy with the sparkling eyes, she thrust open her door and rushed into the road.

"*Don't!*" she shouted.

Nobody paid her attention. Sara grabbed Sterling's arm. "Don't!" she shouted again.

Sterling had his back to her and hadn't seen her coming. He wheeled around. "What the hell?" he demanded.

"Don't!" she said, frantic now. "Don't hit him."

"Hit him?" he asked, surprised.

"He didn't mean anything, I'm sure. The ball wasn't meant to hit the car."

"Don't you think I know that?" Sterling asked. For a long moment he looked at Sara, his eyes narrowed, his expression curious.

"*Señor!*" the boy shouted again.

"Catch, Manuel," Sterling called.

Sara could only watch in wonder as Sterling threw the ball. A minute later they were all throwing and catching, the man, the boy and the children.

Sara moved a few steps away from the game. She was still stunned by the incredible turn of events. She had been so certain Sterling was going to inflict a beating on the boy who had dared to hit his car with a ball. It was what Larry would have done.

Larry.... It didn't take much for Larry to lose his temper. The slightest provocation was enough to set him off. Was it possible that another man could react so differently? Had she forgotten that men could be different from Larry?

After a few minutes, Sterling called, "That's it for now, guys."

There was some animated talk in Spanish. Then Sterling said in English, "Hey, Manuel, want to see what I have for you?"

He went to the back of the car and opened the trunk. As he brought out a bicycle, Sara remembered seeing it when he'd packed the chair.

"*Señor!* You remembered!"

"Didn't think I'd forget, did you?"

Sterling smiled at the boy. That amazingly attractive smile of his in the equally attractive face.

"Oh, *señor!*" Manuel's expression was ecstatic.

"It's not new, Manuel. I bought it from a man whose son has outgrown it. But look, I've put on a new bell and lights, and—"

"A basket over the back wheel! A place for all my stuff."

"That's right. A guy needs a place to put his things."

"Thank you, *señor.* A thousand times, thank you."

"Just one thing, Manuel." Sterling touched the boy's shoulder. "No reckless riding."

"*Señor.*" The boy looked affronted. "As if I would."

Sterling laughed. "I mean it, Manuel. You'll ride on the shoulder of the road, well away from the traffic. I won't have your mother worrying every time you leave the estate. No racing the other cyclists, no stupid tricks."

"I promise, *señor.*"

Manuel rode away, ringing the bell as he went, the other children running fleet-footedly behind him. Sterling was laughing as he got into the car.

Sara hesitated before asking, "The bicycle. Is it a gift?"

"Yes. Why do you ask?"

"I just wondered."

She was thinking what an extraordinarily nice thing Sterling had done for the boy. Thinking, too, that the giving had been so natural, so underplayed. Sterling had class, she acknowledged reluctantly.

"Manuel is a great kid," Sterling said. "His parents have worked for me ever since they came here from Mexico. His father is a field-worker, his mother is my housekeeper. The families of all those kids you just saw live on the estate. Manuel's parents are Spanish-speaking. They know just a few words of English. Manuel is keen about his schoolwork, sees it as his passport to bigger things. The younger kids don't have a problem getting to school. There's a bus that stops just outside the gates. But Manuel goes to a different school, a little farther away. He needs transport."

"And so you arranged it for him."

Sterling shrugged, as if he wondered why she was making such a big deal of the fact.

He was a generous man. But he was still a man, Sara reminded herself. His kindness to the children—and to herself, she acknowledged unwillingly—must not make her forget for one second what men were capable of doing. Any man. All men. Sterling was extraordinarily attractive—but he was still a man.

Minutes later, Sterling stopped the car in front of the lovely house. "Again—welcome to Mountain View," he said.

Close up, the house was even more beautiful than from a distance. For a few seconds, Sara sat motionless and enraptured. But her pleasure vanished instantly when she saw Sterling take her cases from the car.

"This is your home?"

"That's right."

Panic rose in her throat. "I'm not spending the night here with you."

Dark eyes swept Sara's face in a gaze so intense that it brought the blood rushing to her cheeks. "You really are scared of me."

"Scared?" She forced a shrug. "Not scared, Sterling. But there are things I don't do. Where does your regular secretary live?"

"Emma has a house there, in the trees." He motioned with his hand. "The estate office is there, too."

Relief filled Sara at the sight of the two much smaller houses. They were too close to the main house, but at least she and Sterling would not be sharing the same roof.

"You won't need the chair. The house is furnished," Sterling said, as he led the way, "but if you want it, I'll go back for it."

"I won't need it tonight."

His eyes were on her face. She could feel them lingering on her lips. "Certain, then, that you're going back tomorrow?"

The male gaze was unsettling. "Do I have to give you an answer now?"

"I need to know where I stand."

It was so tempting to tell him that she would stay after all in this lovely place. But the gaze that moved down from her face over her throat and then further was intensely disturbing. Sara was accustomed to men. She knew when someone was interested in her. There had been a time when she would be flirting with a man like Sterling, enjoying every moment. But not now. Not anymore. Never again, she told herself fervently. That part of her life was over.

"I think you'll probably have to find yourself someone else," she told him.

At the door of the house, they stopped while Sterling took a bunch of keys from his pocket. Bemused, Sara watched as he selected one and opened the door. Something bothered her, but in her disturbed state she could not have said what it was.

She had no time to register anything about the house as Sterling started down the passage. "I'll take the cases to the bedroom," he said.

Sara found her voice. "Leave them here."

"They're heavy."

"Won't be the first time I've carried them. I'm perfectly

capable of getting them to the bedroom myself—after you've gone.''

"Point taken," Sterling said dryly. "The house is musty, we'll have to open a few windows, get some air into the place.''

"I can do that, too.'' She wasn't certain why she said, "Your secretary, what time does she usually start work?''

His expression didn't change. "Eight-thirty. Does that sound very early to you?''

Sara grimaced. "Work started three hours earlier at the diner. Eight-thirty sounds like luxury to me.''

"Does this mean you're considering the job?''

"I was just interested. Nothing more than that.''

"Just thought I'd ask. Remember, Sara, I will have to know where I stand.''

He grinned at her, his eyes sparkling with mischief. Almost as if he knew what her answer would be—though how could he?

Unconsciously, she took a step toward him, drawn by an instinct that was as old as creation. It was a few moments before she realized what she was doing. If only Sterling wasn't so attractive. Or so sexy. She would have to watch herself—until tomorrow.

"See you in the morning, then," she said coolly.

At the door, Sterling turned. "About supper. You're welcome to join me up at the main house.''

"Thanks, but I don't think so.''

"Fine," he said abruptly. "There should be a few provisions in the kitchen. Nonperishables that Emma left behind. Feel free to help yourself. I'll square things with Emma when she gets back.''

He was walking away when it came to Sara why she'd felt bothered earlier.

"The key," she said, catching up with him. "The key to the house.''

"What about it?''

"I need the key, Sterling.''

Sterling wrinkled his forehead. "Emma's key? She may

have taken it with her. On second thought, she wouldn't have done that. She knew I'd be hiring a replacement. She probably left it in the top kitchen drawer.''

''I need it now, Sterling.''

Sterling's expression changed at her persistence. ''I'm sure you'll find it. But, Sara, Emma has never been one for locking the doors. It's never been necessary out here.''

''All the same.'' Her lips were tight.

''I don't understand. Is it valuables you're worried about? Because if that's it, I can assure you there isn't a dishonest person on this estate.''

''Having watched me pack,'' she said tersely, ''I think you know that I don't have much.''

''Then it's your person.'' His gaze moved over her as it had earlier. ''There are men here who might desire you, but not one of them would dare harm you.''

As before, Sterling's look stirred something inside her, a feeling Sara had not experienced in such a long while. The strangest feeling, entirely at odds with her fear and her resolve that she would never let a man get close to her again.

She lifted her chin. ''I can't take that chance, Sterling. Even if I find Emma's key, I want your key, as well.''

''Good lord! You're asking me for the spare?''

Her cheeks reddened beneath a gaze that had suddenly turned mocking, but she managed to keep her eyes steady. ''That's it.''

''Do you think I'm going to creep into the house when you're not looking?'' Dark eyes taunted her. ''You can't really think that.''

''I'm just asking for the key, Sterling.''

''You said you can take care of yourself, Sara.''

This was proving more difficult than she'd anticipated. Sara's fingers curled into her palms, the nails biting into the soft skin. ''That's right.''

''I know how you feel about being touched. How about if I give you my word that nothing will happen to you?''

Larry could have said those same words, and there was

a time when she'd have taken them on trust. It had taken
a while—too long—for Sara to discover that Larry had a
talent for looking a person in the eye and lying outra-
geously at the same time. Although superficially Sterling
could not be more different from Larry, Sara had learned
at great cost that appearances were deceptive. She had no
reason to trust a man she had only known a few hours.

She barely controlled a shiver. "I just need to be certain
that I have all the keys in my possession," she said icily.

"Meaning you're unwilling to take my word."

"I'm sorry you insist on putting it that way." Sara's
cheeks were warm. "I don't mean to be rude, and it isn't
personal."

She braced herself for self-righteous anger, a calculated
show of disappointment and resentment, all meant to un-
dermine her defenses.

But Sterling only said, "Seems to me you're thinking
of leaving tomorrow."

"I still have to get through tonight. I'll give back the
key when I go."

Sterling was studying her again, his expression enigmatic. Sara would have given a lot to know what he was
thinking.

After a few seconds he dropped his gaze. Sara let out
a breath of relief when he took the ring of keys from his
pocket, slipped one off and gave it to her.

She watched as the tall, broad-shouldered man strode
lithely away, shivering as she thought about the effect he
was starting to have on her. His vibrant sexuality was
enormously exciting. But there was another side of him,
too—humor and intelligence coupled with compassion.
The combination made him unbelievably attractive.

There had been a time—in an era long past—when Sara
had enjoyed the company of attractive men. Passionate
and sensuous, she had been able to sense those qualities
in some of the men she met. Yet until Larry, she had never
progressed beyond kissing and flirting, for despite the pas-

sionate side of her nature, Sara had been old-fashioned enough to believe that she would never give herself to a man until she knew she was in love.

The memory of their first meeting was still vivid. With her sights firmly set on an advertising career, she had been thrilled to find an opening in the large Maine company in which her father had worked for so long. Advertising was Dad's passion, and it soon became Sara's, too.

When she was asked by Larry, a rising star in the company, to prepare a presentation for a new computer game, she had put all her efforts into the task. He had praised her presentation effusively and asked her to have a drink with him afterward. Next day, he asked her to have dinner with him and sent flowers to her home.

Sara had believed herself in love with Larry, and at first things had been wonderful between them. Larry had wooed her with flowers and chocolates, midnight calls and visits to the kinds of places she would never have been able to afford herself. Every day, her defenses had been undermined.

Laughing Larry, they called him, the people who did not know the true nature of the man. He was so handsome, so exuberantly boyish, he was everything a woman could wish for in a man—or so Sara had thought. He was such fun, quick to flirt and flatter and generous to a fault. The moment came when Sara no longer wished to resist him and agreed to move in with him.

The changes came slowly. A temper tantrum one day, a hard slap across the face another. Always afterward came the apologies, abject and heartfelt. "Stay with me, Sara. I love you, darling, don't ever leave me." And then gifts and promises never to hurt her again.

At first, Sara had been so deeply in love that she had allowed Larry to hurt her. Fool that she'd been. She knew that now. Over and over, she asked herself why she had stayed with him for so long.

She had, in fact, tried to leave more than once. Each time Larry had threatened to have her father fired from

the company and blacklisted from others of the same kind.
Her parents had fallen on rough times. They needed the
money that came with her father's income as a graphic
artist. Besides, after almost thirty years, the company was
Dad's life. Sara knew she could not let Larry carry out
his threats.

And so she remained with him, suffering his increasing
abuse and his blackmail, trying to believe him whenever
he apologized and promised not to hurt her again. Hoping
each time that he meant what he said. Until the last time,
when she understood that she had to get away no matter
what.

If only she could leave Larry in the past, she thought.
Yet with all that had happened, he would never really be
gone from her life, for he had destroyed an innate part of
her that had once been precious. Her reaction to Sterling,
her fear of being touched, her absolute determination
never to allow any man to grow close to her again—to
hurt her—told her that.

Still, she had to stop thinking about Larry. If she didn't,
she would go mad.

Sara became aware of something cold and hard in her
hand. She was still holding the key. It was time to go
inside and take a look at her new, if very temporary, home.

She saw almost immediately why the old chair was not
needed here. The house was small yet compact and taste-
fully furnished. The living room was bright and colorful,
with woven rugs on the floor, two comfortable love seats,
a couple of lamps, some pictures and a TV. The kitchen
was small, too, but fitted with lots of cupboards.

In the bedroom, Sara drew in a breath of pure pleasure.
The room was quite different from the one she had so
recently vacated, spacious and airy, with a large window
giving on to a view of the hills. A brightly colored patch-
work quilt covered the bed, and on the bureau stood a
ceramic vase filled with dried flowers.

A person could be happy in this house, Sara thought.
She could be happy here.

If only Sterling, sexy and far too attractive Sterling, had no part in the marvelous picture that was the Mountain View Wine Estate. But Sterling owned the estate, and Sara had as much as told him she was only staying the night.

Going to the kitchen, she realized she was hungry for the first time that day. Remembering that Sterling had told her to help herself, she opened the refrigerator. It was almost empty, but in the grocery cupboard Sara found crackers and a few cans of soup.

Earlier, in the restaurant with Sterling, she had been unable to eat. Alone in the quiet kitchen, with a hot bowl of soup and a handful of crackers, she couldn't remember the last time food had tasted so good.

Later, much later, Sara studied herself in the full-length bedroom mirror. She put both hands beneath her breasts, then moved her hands slowly over her stomach.

Still flat, she told herself. Nothing visible—at least, not yet. True, her breasts were a little fuller than they had been, but it would be some time before her pregnancy showed. Only the most perceptive stranger would suspect anything. Certainly, it was unlikely to occur to Sterling that Sara was pregnant.

She gave a little moan as her hand stroked the line of her stomach and she imagined the baby that was beginning to take shape deep inside her. A baby conceived not in love or passion, but as the result of force.

She remembered the night Larry had come home reeking of liquor and stale perfume. She should have known better than to taunt him about having another woman. The words had been a goad, driving him to demand sex with Sara. She refused, upon which he proceeded to force her.

Next day, Sara packed a suitcase. When she told Larry she was leaving, he threatened—again—to have her father fired. Reluctantly, she agreed to stay.

A short time later, she knew she was pregnant. Larry went ballistic when he learned the news. It was all Sara's fault, he shouted. She'd known from the start that he had

no intention of being a father. She should have taken care
it did not happen. She was mistaken if she thought she
could force him into marriage.

"You'll have an abortion." He was adamant.

"No!"

Though she had not wanted a baby, Sara knew she
would do nothing to get rid of it.

"It's an order, Sara. I'll speak to someone tomorrow.
You'll have it done right away."

"No way," she told him defiantly.

Larry stared at her, enraged, a bull thwarted by a lowly
matador waving a taunting red flag. Breathing hard, Sara
stared at him, wondering what had happened to the sweet
boyishness she had once loved in him. There was no trace
of it now.

Without warning, Larry lunged at her, punching her
hard in the stomach. Again and again, he hit her.

"I'm leaving," she told him when she could talk. "This
time you won't stop me." Fury gave her the strength to
stand up to him, despite the fact that he would probably
hit her again.

"Like hell I can't stop you!" he shouted. "You'll go
nowhere, Sara. If I can't have you, nobody will. I'll kill
you rather than let you go to another man. And you will
not have this baby."

Sara did not answer him. That night she lay awake,
thinking of her parents. She couldn't stay any longer with
Larry, not with a baby to consider.

She was tempted to tell her parents the truth before she
left Maine. But she understood her father well enough to
know that if he learned about the abuse and the blackmail,
he would confront Larry in a rage. He would say things
that Larry would never forgive, do things that would never
be forgotten. And then where would he be? It was possible
that Larry's threats to have her father fired had been idle,
but if Dad acted in temper, his job would be terminated
on the spot, and Sara's long sacrifice would have been
in vain.

Next day, when Larry was out of the way, she hurriedly packed the two suitcases. She did not know where she would go, only that it would be far from Maine, a place where Larry would never find her.

She wrote her parents a note, telling them only that she was leaving town and not to worry about her. She would write or call when she could. She mailed the note after leaving the apartment.

Riding trains and buses, she found her way to the small California town. Once there, she discovered that finding a job was not as easy as she had imagined. Knowing Larry as well as she did, she understood that she could not approach an advertising agency for fear that he would discover her whereabouts. She also learned that if she wanted an office job, she needed references. For the same reason, she could not acquire them.

When she saw the Help Wanted notice in the window of Big Bill's diner, she considered herself lucky to find a room and a job.

Once more, Sara's hands went to her stomach. It wasn't the baby's fault that its father was Larry. Sara had always adored children. Now that she was going to be a mother, she knew she would love her baby as much as she could possibly love any child despite the way in which it had been conceived. Already she was developing a protective, maternal feeling toward the tiny being inside her.

That was why, in the months ahead, she had to build up some savings and find a permanent home. Sara was determined that her baby, the baby she loved long before it was born, would want for nothing. She would make certain her child had the best life she could provide for it.

CHAPTER THREE

EARLY the next morning, Sara saw a note lying on the floor just beside the front door.

"Help yourself to food in the main house. Feel free to raid the refrigerator and the grocery cupboard. Front door open. S."

A brief note, the script big and strong, like its writer, the words casual and generous. Sara had glimpsed that generosity yesterday in Sterling's dealings with Manuel and the children. The words and writing belonged to a strong, independent and confident man.

She hadn't been awake long. Her first reaction on opening her eyes to unfamiliar surroundings had been confusion—*Where am I?*—but it had taken just a few seconds for memory to return. The next question had come quickly. *What now?*

Holding the note, she went to the bedroom. But instead of choosing fresh clothes and heading for the shower, she went to the open window.

Leaning her elbows on the sill, she let her eyes feast on the vista of vineyards that extended toward the mist-covered hills and the mountains beyond.

And then a man came into view, and something tightened inside her. His back was to her as he walked toward the vineyards, two dogs bounding at his heels.

Sara was aware that more than a few men were employed at Mountain View, and in jeans, a plaid shirt and a big hat, he could be anyone. But there was something about the broad shoulders and narrow hips, the loose yet powerful stride that struck a chord deep inside her. She knew the man was Sterling.

Sara watched a few seconds longer, wishing she could

be walking through the vineyards at Sterling's side. And then she thought of Larry and all that had happened to her, and she turned from the window abruptly.

When she had showered and dressed, she left the room. What now? Yesterday she had threatened to leave the estate, but she had been speaking out of bravado and on impulse. The reality was that she had no job and, because of the danger posed by Larry, not even the prospect of one. It would be months before she would risk looking for work in her field. Of course, there was always Paula's offer of help, something to fall back on if she was helpless or desperate.

But Sara had no intention of being desperate or helpless. Not now, not ever again.

Some time during the night, it had come to her that she could function perfectly well on her own. She might ask Paula to put her up for a night or two until she found another restaurant job. Or perhaps she might find house-keeping work in one of the many bed-and-breakfast places she had glimpsed on the way to the wine estate. But one way or another, she would take care of herself and her baby.

Away from Larry's abusiveness, from Big Bill's crude and bullying tactics, Sara understood that she was her own person. She did not have to put up with abuse, threats or blackmail from anyone.

Her thoughts turned to food. Miracle of miracles, she was hungry. After a few weeks of early-morning nausea, she craved a cup of coffee and a slice of toast. Things were looking up!

There was coffee in the grocery cupboard, but Emma's refrigerator held neither bread nor milk. Longingly, Sara looked at Sterling's note. There was no danger of meeting him, for he was safely in the vineyards, and the invitation had been issued sincerely, she felt sure of it.

Her spirits lifted as she walked to the main house. Later it would be hot, but so early in the morning it was still cool, and the grass was damp underfoot. The air was sweet and rang with the sound of bird song. On all sides were the vineyards, acres upon acres of vines. And beyond them were the hills.

Oh, but this place was beautiful. More beautiful than she had imagined yesterday when Sterling had mentioned it in the restaurant.

The front door of the house was open. Sterling must be a trusting person, Sara thought, as she went inside. Walking past the living room, she saw a wooden-beamed ceiling and wide windows, furniture that was light and low and long-lined and several shelves of books. It was a wonderful room, rustic and inviting.

In the kitchen, she was delighted to see a percolator, hot and filled almost to the brim with coffee. She felt a little awkward about opening the refrigerator to look for milk, but Sterling had said to help herself, and so she did. She also found crusty bread and a thick wedge of cheese.

As she sat in an alcove dining area, Sara was amazed at how hungry she was. She sipped her coffee slowly, looking about. The kitchen, like the living room, was inviting, nicely laid out and functional. A kitchen made for a woman who loved to cook.

"Good morning."

"Sterling!"

"Glad to see you do eat sometimes."

"My third slice of toast." She smiled at him. "You'll be sorry you gave me the run of your supplies."

"Actually, I was beginning to wonder what you survive on. Shall I put another slice in the toaster?"

"Heavens, no! I'll turn into a pig if I eat any more."

"You're so thin, it would take more than a bit of toast to fatten you up."

Little did he know that in a few months she would be enormous.

"Well, Sara—are you going to have that extra slice?"

He smiled as she shook her head, the smile she remembered from yesterday. Oh, but he was attractive! And so sexy, the most sexually appealing man she had ever met, was ever likely to meet. Somewhere deep in the core of her being, something stirred and flamed, but it was a sensation she had to ignore. Larry's sex appeal had led to disaster. She was never going to let that happen again.

"I want to ask you something." Her voice was low as she tried not to let her nervousness show.

Watchful eyes held hers. "Ask away."

"Yesterday... I didn't think I would stay." She forced herself not to look away from him. "What would you say if I changed my mind?"

"That would depend," Sterling said lazily, "on why you changed it."

She was taken aback by the answer. "Does it matter?"

"Yes, Sara, I think it does."

So Sterling had no intention of making it easy for her. He wanted to see her squirm. In the end, he was no different from other men. Briefly, anger flared.

"What do you want?" she asked tersely. "A treatise? Seven double-spaced pages on why I want to work at Mountain View Wine Estate?"

Dark eyes sparkled. "Nothing as awful as that. Just an explanation that satisfies me. Yesterday you were adamant about leaving. You can't blame me for wanting to know— why the change of mind?"

Couldn't the man say, "I need a secretary—you'll do until Emma gets back"? But it seemed he could not.

"If you don't want me here, just say so," she snapped.

"I need an explanation, and you're being evasive."

Sara lifted her head. "Perhaps because you are arrogant and persistent."

Sterling threw back his head and laughed. "Arrogant? Because I want to know something about an extremely mysterious woman?"

"I don't have to take this," she told him.

"No, you don't," he agreed. "And I can have you driven back to town whenever you're ready."

His meaning couldn't have been clearer.

Unhappily, Sara looked at Sterling. It should have been

so easy to tell him of Larry's blackmail and abuse, of her pregnancy and her desperate need for a temporary refuge. But that would mean seeing pity in Sterling's eyes. She couldn't bear that. Anything but pity.

Yet if she wanted to remain here—and she did, very much—she had to say something.

"This is a beautiful place." The words came slowly.

"And?"

"Does there have to be an and?"

"You know there does."

Damn the man! His relentlessness was beginning to get to her.

"It suits me to be here. Away from…" She stopped.

"From a situation you don't like very much," he finished for her.

She jerked her head. "I didn't say that."

"You didn't have to. Sara, I asked you yesterday if you were on the run."

She shouldn't be surprised he was perceptive, for the dark eyes shone with lively intelligence. Sterling Tayler was not a man to be put off easily with evasions.

"Perhaps there was a situation," she said tightly, "but it has nothing to do with you."

"Maybe it does."

"No!" A hand knocked her mug sideways as she stood up. "And maybe this really is a mistake."

Sterling moved the mug away from the edge of the table. "Sara—this is the same scenario we went through yesterday."

"Only because you *insist* on knowing things that have nothing to do with you." She looked at him, unaware that her face was very pale, her eyes even more haunted than usual. "Isn't it enough that I want to be here? That I need a job—badly? That I need a salary and a place to live?"

Quietly, he said, "Are things really as bad as that?"

With a dry throat, she said, "Yes."

"But you don't want to talk about it."

"No." She looked past him, through the window, toward the hills. In a low voice she went on. "I haven't robbed a bank or mugged anyone. I haven't committed a crime. I haven't done a thing that can get you into trouble. You wouldn't be harboring a criminal."

Something moved in Sterling's jaw. He took a step toward her, his hands reaching for her face. Without thinking, she moved toward him. For a moment she longed to feel his fingers on her cheeks and in her hair.

And then she remembered, and she jerked away from him. "No!"

"Sorry." His expression was unreadable.

"It mustn't happen again."

"I can't promise you that."

"Sterling... Sterling, you have to."

"You're a woman, and I'm a man, Sara, and that makes promises difficult to keep. You don't know a thing if you don't know that."

There was something dark and dangerous about him in that moment. Over the hard-beating pulse in her throat, Sara said, "Obviously, it's best if I go."

Lazily, Sterling said, "Pity, because I was about to tell you to stay."

Sara closed her eyes for a second. She felt relief yet she wondered if she had already said too much.

"Don't fight it, Sara," he said, as if he knew how difficult the issue had become for her. "It's okay if you just say yes. You don't have to say more than that."

The perilous moment had passed, and she could savor the relief.

"One condition, Sterling. Despite what you just said. No liberties."

"What happened just now wasn't a liberty, only a gesture."

"Whatever it was, it was too much."

He looked at her curiously. "Such a small thing, Sara. Just a touch on the cheek."

"It's not small to me," she muttered.

"A beautiful woman... And so untouched." He put out

a hand again, then dropped it to his side. "Have you never been kissed?"

"Don't," she said.

"I'm just asking, Sara. A woman as lovely as you—the men must be fighting to be with you."

"No." Her voice was choked.

"It's hard for me to believe that you've never had a man in your life. Or that you're so frightened of men. Of sex." His expression turned thoughtful. "Has there been a man, Sara? Is that what this is all about? Is there someone in your past? Someone who frightened you?"

She didn't owe him any explanations. Her private life was her own. But he was getting too close to the truth, and she couldn't allow that.

Deliberately, Sara said, "I'm not interested in sex. The mere thought of being touched turns me off. Isn't that enough for you?" She was well aware that she hadn't answered his question.

Sterling was quiet a long moment. At last he said, "If it has to be. But, Sara, I have a condition, too."

She looked at him warily. "Oh?"

"Two, actually."

"You didn't say anything about conditions earlier."

"I am now." His tone was cool and matter-of-fact. "You'll need to make a commitment."

"A commitment?"

"Right. None of this telling me one moment that you're going, the next that you're staying. I run a busy wine estate. I have supplies coming in all the time, orders to get out. We have tours and wine tastings several times a week, and you'll have to help out with those. I don't have time for all this shilly-shallying."

"Wine tastings?" Her interest was stirred. "First time you've mentioned them."

"We never did go into much detail about your duties, but I'm telling you now."

"I like wine, but I don't know much about it."

"Are you willing to learn?"

"Yes, of course!"

His expression changed. "I'll teach you."

"What else will I do, Sterling?"

"As I told you yesterday, some bookkeeping and correspondence."

"Shouldn't be a problem." For once it was easy to smile at him.

"Then you really have worked in an office." It was a statement, not a question.

"Yes. I think I said so yesterday."

"You didn't tell me what you were doing in the diner. Especially when you weren't much good as a waitress."

"It was all I could get at the time," she said simply.

Sterling's expression showed that her explanation didn't satisfy him, but as if he realized he was entering forbidden territory, he didn't press her.

Instead, he said, "I still need that commitment. Emma will be away two months. I have to be certain you'll stay till she gets back."

A two-month breathing space. Time in which to save some money. A lovely house to live in. Beautiful surroundings. What more could she want?

"Sara." Sterling's voice jerked her out of her thoughts. "You seemed so far away just then. Is there a problem?"

"No. And you do have my commitment."

"And then there's the second condition. Never lie to me, Sara."

"Lie?" she asked, a little shakily.

Thoughtful eyes rested on her face, lingered for a long moment on trembling lips. "You have to be honest with me. At all times."

He was talking about her new duties, of course, and she knew that she would be honest in anything that concerned the wine estate. Her private life was a different matter. Even Sterling could not expect her to talk about Larry.

"Do we have an agreement, Sara?"

"Yes."

"Let's shake on it," he said, and held out his hand to her.

Swallowing hard, Sara made herself take the big hand. It held hers a few seconds longer than necessary, and she wasn't at all surprised when a shiver ran through her wrist and up her arm.

As she snatched her hand away, she felt, inexplicably, as if she had been burned where he'd touched her. This was unbelievable! She had fancied herself in love with Larry. Their relationship had been very much more intimate than a formal handshake, and yet she couldn't remember ever feeling like this. The sensation was new to her.

"There it is." Her voice shook. "An agreement."

"An agreement," Sterling echoed. His lips were tilted very lightly at the corners, and his eyes, those wonderful dark eyes, held an expression that was intensely disturbing.

"When...when do I start?" The words came out in a whisper because her throat was so dry.

God, but this was awful! Independent, assertive Sara, turned to jelly by a momentary, and very formal, touch of a man's hand. The sooner she got a grip on herself the better.

She swallowed hard. In a louder voice, she said, "When did you say Emma left?"

"I didn't. She's been gone almost a week."

"With the original replacement letting you down, there must be a ton of work for me to do by now."

"A fair bit."

"Why don't I start immediately?"

"Aren't you the eager beaver, Sara?" Sterling grinned at her. "I was about to have some coffee. Pour yourself another cup."

"I never have more than one. So if you don't mind, I'll just go and—"

"Join me anyway. I'll tell you a little about your duties. And after that I'll show you around the wineries."

* * *

Sara had never been inside a winery before, and she was fascinated.

The first thing that struck her as they entered the huge building, was the odor. Fermentation, Sterling told her, laughing as he saw her wrinkling her nose.

"Fermentation?" She was eager to know everything.

"Right, and in time I'll take you through the whole wine-making process. For now, I just want to show you around the place."

They went first to the cellars, and Sara shivered as she was hit by the unexpected chill.

"Aging wine needs to be kept cold," Sterling explained, "which is why we keep this part of the process underground." And then he added, "I should have told you to bring a sweater."

"I'm okay." But Sara was shivering.

"This isn't a pass," Sterling said, as his arm went around her.

"Sterling…"

"Body heat helps stave off the cold."

He was holding her so close that she fitted snugly into the hollow of his armpit. The feel of his body, the hard lines of his chest, the tautness of his thighs, evoked an excitement that intensified her shivering.

"You really are cold," he said contritely, and she didn't dispute the statement.

The strangest things were happening to her. Her brain was sending out contradictory signals. It was telling the reasoning part of her to get away from Sterling while she could, yet refusing to give her limbs the power to move.

Sterling was speaking again, and Sara tried to force herself—not altogether successfully—to concentrate on his words rather than his body. He showed her the enormous oak barrels where the wine was kept and the hoses that ran across the ceiling and pumped the mature wine into the rest of the wineries.

When they emerged from the cellars, Sterling was still holding her. It was a minute at least before Sara registered that fact, it felt so good to be close to his body. She moved away from him quickly.

Darting a look at Sterling, she saw the quizzical lifting of brows, the sparkle in his eyes, and she knew that he had not been unaware of her reaction in the cellars. As she deliberately increased the distance between them, Sara thought—though she could not be certain—that she heard a low chuckle. Hateful man!

"Quite a place you have here." Her voice was as matter-of-fact as she could make it.

"You haven't seen most of it yet."

He showed her the crushers in which the harvested grapes were crushed and the tanks in which they were fermented. He led her from one mechanized operation to another—the plant where bottles were being filled with dark red wine, the machine where the bottles were corked and another where bottle after bottle was affixed with the Mountain View label.

At every step of the process people stood watching, making certain that the machines were functioning properly. Sterling spoke to everyone and introduced Sara as the new secretary.

Emerging from the wine-processing part of the building, they came to the gift store. Sara looked around, enchanted. There were arrays of different wines, some of them wrapped in cellophane and tied with colorful ribbons. There were the white wines, Rieslings and Chenins and Chardonnays. And the reds, Pinot Noir and Beaujolais and cabernet sauvignon. There were exotic specialty bottles made in different shapes. One bottle looked like a violin, another like a bunch of grapes. Gift baskets tempted the eye, baskets filled with wine and cheese and pretty glasses.

"This is where the wine tasting takes place," Sterling said as they came to a table that held a collection of small glasses. "We're not expecting any tours today, but before they arrive, we put out platters of cheese and crackers and carafes filled with our different wines."

"And people sample them?"

"That's right, and more often than not, they go away buying a wine that pleases them."

"I had no idea it was going to be anything like this," Sara said.

Sterling grinned at her "You haven't even seen the place where the whole process begins. The vineyards."

"I can't wait to see them."

"I'll take you on a tour tomorrow or the next day." Sterling picked up a glass. "Your own private wine tasting, Sara. What would you like to sample first? White or red?"

She was about to tell him her preference for red wine when a snippet of information she had once read came back to her. Alcohol during pregnancy might not be good for the baby.

"Actually," Sara said, "I don't think I'll have any."

His eyebrows lifted. "You don't like wine?"

"Only occasionally. And not right now, Sterling."

"Wine and sex—I'll have to educate you in the pleasures of living, Sara."

She backed away from him. "I'd rather you didn't."

"A joke," he said mildly. "But here's a thought. If you won't taste the wine, how will you handle the wine tastings?"

She lifted her chin at him. "It won't be a problem."

They were leaving the wineries when Sterling asked Sara what she intended doing about meals.

"You're welcome to eat with me."

"Thanks, but I don't think so."

"Manuel's mother is a good cook."

"I'm sure she is, but I like eating alone."

"Now why doesn't that surprise me?" he responded sarcastically.

She refused to let his displeasure affect her. "What does Emma do about food? And the other workers?"

"There's a small town not far from the estate," he answered her shortly. "You can get most things you'll need there. You didn't see it yesterday. I can drive you there later."

"If you'll tell me how to get there, I could go myself."

Sterling's lips tightened. "I'm not a demon, Sara."

"If I thought you were," she said firmly, "I wouldn't have agreed to work for you. Sterling... Please understand, this isn't personal, but I have to be independent. It's really important to me."

For a long moment Sterling didn't answer her. He only looked at her from his great height, his eyes subjecting her face to an intense searching, as if he was trying to see through the surface to the very core of her, to understand the things she wasn't telling him. Tension coiled inside her.

"Do you drive?" he asked at last.

Sara nodded.

"Fine. I'll let you take a car and give you directions."

"Thanks. Am I going to see the office, Sterling?"

"I'll take you there now."

Sara spent the rest of the morning in the estate office, getting to know the computer, the filing system, reading some of the correspondence. An office was her working world, as the restaurant had not been, and this office was especially pleasant. The computer was fairly new, the word-processing system one with which Sara was familiar. The chair and desk had been chosen with an eye to a secretary's comfort. On the walls were colorful posters picturing grapes and wine bottles. She couldn't have found a nicer place in which to spend the next two months.

Later that day, she borrowed an estate car and followed Sterling's instructions to the town. Cyclists were everywhere on the roads, and hot-air balloons floated over the valley. The town was small and quaint, with oak-lined streets and colorful houses.

Sara had just parked the car near a supermarket when someone called, "Hey, *señorita! Señorita* Sara!"

Looking around in surprise, she saw Manuel barreling

down the street on his new bicycle, waving to her as he approached.

"How's the bike?" she asked, as he stopped beside her and swung his leg over the bar to the ground.

"Pretty neat," he told her, the American words sounding picturesque in the soft Mexican accent. "No problem to go to school now."

"You must be glad Sterling gave it to you."

Dark eyes rolled upward. "Very glad. The *señor* is one neat man. Best man in California."

"You haven't met all the others," Sara told him, laughing.

"I don't have to. I know what I know. You go to buy groceries, *señorita?* I will help you."

Manuel locked his bicycle to a bike stand and led the way into the supermarket. Half an hour later, groceries stowed in the car, they went to an ice-cream parlor where Sara treated Manuel to an ice cream. Manuel bolted his ice cream before making inroads on Sara's helping, which she was suddenly too nauseous to eat.

"The town is bigger than I realized," she marveled as they left the ice-cream parlor. "Isn't that a library across the street there?"

"With every book in the world," Manuel told her solemnly.

"Not *every* book, surely," she teased.

"Maybe not every one. But many, many." Another rolling of the liquid dark eyes. "More books than any one person can read. And newspapers, *señorita.* Papers from all over the United States."

"Really? I find that hard to believe."

"For the tourists," he told her. "They come to California to vacation, but they want news of home."

Interesting, Sara thought. She would have to go to the library now and then. The Napa Valley was an ideal refuge, but there would be times when she would be homesick for Maine. If she was lucky she would find a paper with news of her home state.

*   *   *

Before driving back to Mountain View, she went to a public phone and called her parents.

"Sara! Where are you?" Her mother sounded anxious, yet relieved to hear her voice.

"I can't tell you, Mom, but I'm fine."

"Darling, we're all frantic. We don't understand why you took off so suddenly."

Sara's throat was raw with unshed tears. "I'm sorry… Mom, didn't you get my note?"

"Yes, and there was that one phone call a few days later, but you didn't explain anything. Where are you, darling? Please, you must tell me."

"Mom…" Sara paused, tempted to give her mother at least a bit of information. She could ask for her confidence, plead with her to keep her whereabouts secret.

"Larry is frantic, too. He's on to your father every day, wanting to know if we've heard from you. He wants you to come home, Sara. We all want you back."

So Larry was frantic. Sara could just imagine. Larry's frantic state stemmed from his fury at being thwarted. At that moment, she understood that she could not tell her mother her whereabouts. If she did, it would be just a matter of time before Larry came chasing after her.

"Mom," she said quietly, "I called because I wanted you to know I'm okay. Please, don't ask me more than that."

"Larry is determined to get you back. He says he'll do whatever it takes to find you."

An icy shiver ran down Sara's spine.

"I'll come back when the time is right," she said, as calmly as she was able.

"Sara!" Her father's voice. She had forgotten this was his day off from work. He must have heard her mother talking and picked up one of the extensions. "Sara, what are we to tell Larry? He's like a crazy man. You never saw anything like it."

Crazy man was right. Larry was indeed crazy, but not in the way her parents imagined.

"Don't tell him anything," she pleaded. "Don't even tell him I called."

"Where are you?" asked her father. "You have to tell us."

"Dad, I can't."

"We can have the call traced."

"No, I'm calling from a public phone. Mom, Dad… Oh, God, I love you both so much. Leaving home had nothing to do with you, please believe that."

"Sara." Her mother was crying.

"I have to go," she said, and put down the receiver before they could hear her tears.

The nightmare began soon after she fell asleep.

Larry was hurting her. The reason wasn't clear, but he was yelling at her, pushing her head against the wall. She was screaming at him to stop. But he went on.

When she thought she couldn't bear the torment a moment longer, he pushed her to the ground. The hands that gripped her breasts were claws with nails like talons. His legs were steel rods, wrapping themselves around her so tightly that she couldn't move. His mouth was a hundred times the size of a normal mouth, sucking her in, devouring her inch by inch. His body was a lead weight, crushing the breath in her lungs.

"No!" Sara screamed. "No, Larry, no! Leave me! Larry, no! No, no, no!"

The nightmare worsened as a second pair of arms gripped her. "Sara, Sara…" The owner of the new arms was calling her name.

"No! Oh, God, no!" She lashed against this new assailant, fighting to get away from him. He was different in some way, more substantial.

"Sara! Sara, you're dreaming."

She shook her head violently. "I'm not dreaming! Leave me, Larry, leave me!" She was sobbing.

But he didn't leave her, this new person with arms that

were surprisingly warm where they touched her skin. The first set of arms were so cold.

"You're dreaming," an insistent voice said. "Sara, wake up!"

Slowly Larry's image began to fade, and the monstrous body with its larger-than-life limbs disintegrated. But there was this other person holding her against him.

"Wake up," he said again.

She was sobbing, her breath coming in great gasps. Her body was bathed in sweat. The brutality had gone, but elements of the nightmare persisted. Yet for some reason she was unable to go on fighting.

She didn't resist as the large man holding her stroked her damp hair and wiped her wet face. All the while he talked to her softly, telling her she'd been dreaming, that she had nothing to worry about, that she was safe.

Safe... Oh, God, if only he knew. She would never feel safe again.

Still, she was beginning to feel a little better, comforted in a strange sort of way. As he went on stroking her—she knew it wasn't Larry—she allowed herself to relax against him. She wasn't thinking as she sobbed quietly and let him stroke her hair.

Somewhere on the very fringes of her consciousness, she was enjoying the warmth of the male body, the rhythm of the stroking movement. Gradually, a strange excitement invaded her, a longing for the warm body to remain close to hers, for the stroking to go on forever.

At length, her sobbing lessened. Eventually she grew still. For at least a minute she was motionless, scarcely breathing.

And then Sterling said, "Sara? Are you okay?"

She stiffened. "What do you mean?"

"You had a nightmare. A bad one. But you're out of it now."

Gentle words, gently spoken. But she couldn't let herself be duped or lulled. For Larry had been gentle, too, at the start, when he was trying to get her into his bed. At the time, she'd been foolish enough to believe that he loved her. But Larry's gentleness had been a façade.

And Sterling, this big, tough man who had inserted himself into her life yesterday morning and taken charge in his macho way, was showing an amazing gentleness. In Sara's loneliness and despair, it was tempting to let herself be taken in by him. But wouldn't he, too, take advantage of her if she did?

"No!" Suddenly, she was struggling against him once more.

His arm tightened around her. "It's over, Sara. Don't you know that?"

Pushing her fists hard against his chest, she shouted fiercely, "You don't know what you're talking about!"

"You were just dreaming, Sara."

"*This* is not a dream."

"No, it's all over now, and you're okay." His voice had changed, as if he wondered why she was acting so strangely.

"You're wrong, the nightmare isn't over," she whispered. "It will never be over."

His hand left her hair and went to her face, trailing a sensuous path across her cheeks, then her lips. "Sara…"

His touch was doing the strangest things to her senses, exciting her and frightening her at the same time. Larry and Sterling. Two such different men, arousing such different sensations in her. Yet both men were cut from the same basic cloth. *Didn't she know that now?*

"No!" Her voice rose. "No! No! No!" With all her strength she pushed at him. "Get your hands off me, Sterling."

After a moment, he did. Dropping his hands—how cold she felt where his fingers had been—he released her and stood up. "At least you know who I am now."

"What…what do you mean?"

"I'm not some guy called Larry."

A shivering started deep inside her. For a moment she couldn't speak.

"You had a nightmare, but it's time you came out of it. No nightmare lasts this long."

"You don't know a damn thing about it!" She bit the words out harshly.

"Come on, Sara, it's just taking you exceptionally long to get over it."

"Not a damn thing!" she repeated.

Sterling took a step away from the bed. "Look, why don't I bring you something to drink? A cup of tea? You'd like that, wouldn't you?"

"Maybe..." Tea sounded tempting.

"Do you have any here? I know you bought supplies today. Otherwise I'll go get a tea bag from the main house."

"There's tea in the cupboard," Sara muttered.

A moment later it came to her that letting this man make her tea could be construed as a sign of weakness. Sitting up straight, she said, "I'll do it myself."

He pushed her gently back against the pillows. "Don't be an idiot. Milk? Sugar?"

She gave in reluctantly. "A little milk."

It was only when Sterling had left the room that Sara wondered for the first time how he had managed to enter the house.

"How did you get in?" she demanded when he returned, carrying a steaming mug. "I locked the door before I went to bed, I could swear to it."

"The side door," Sterling said.

So much for the security of a lock. "There's a side door?" Sara asked, shocked.

"Next to the kitchen. You might not have noticed it."

She had seen a door, Sara remembered. She'd taken it for a storage closet. It hadn't occurred to her to open it, to see where it led.

"Why didn't you give me the key to that door, as well?"

Sterling frowned. "There must have been one once. I

don't know if there is now. At any rate, the door was unlocked.''

''How convenient,'' Sara sneered. ''You'll be telling me next you didn't think about it until now.''

The eyes that met hers were confident and self-assured. ''That's exactly it.''

''I need a key for that door, Sterling. If you don't have one, I'll call in a locksmith and have one made. I take it there's a locksmith in the town?''

''Manuel's father will make it for you. And in case you're wondering whether he'll make a duplicate—he's not that kind.''

''All men are that kind,'' Sara said flatly.

''Do you really think that?''

''I know it,'' she said feelingly.

Sterling walked to the window and stood with his back to her. Tensely Sara watched him, taking in every inch of the wide shoulders, the strong thrust of his throat.

When he turned, the set of his mouth was firm, his eyes shuttered. ''You distrust men so deeply. Is that why you don't want to be touched?''

''Don't analyze me, Sterling,'' Sara said shortly. ''And about the side door—I'll be putting a chair in front of it until I have a key.''

Sterling gave a hard, mirthless laugh. ''You have some chip on that very slender shoulder.''

''You can go now.'' Her lifted chin presented a show of composure she was far from feeling.

An unexpected glimmer of amusement touched his eyes. ''Here's your tea.''

She took the mug he held out to her and cradled it between her hands. The perspiration had dried on her body, and she felt cold.

''Please go,'' she said.

But Sterling ignored the request and sat in the chair by the bed. ''What was the nightmare about?''

Sara stiffened. ''It was just a dream.''

''An unusually vivid dream. What was it about?''

"You know how it is with dreams." She tried to speak casually. "You forget them the moment you wake up."

"But you haven't forgotten this one, Sara. You said it would never end."

She *had* said it. How stupid of her. Now he wouldn't let the matter rest.

"You took so long to get out of it. So what was it about, Sara?"

Playing for time, she took a sip from the mug. The tea felt so good going down her parched throat.

And all the while, Sterling was watching her. When a minute had passed, he said, "Sara?"

She looked away from him. "I don't want to talk about it."

"Somebody was hurting you."

She hesitated. "You could be right."

"Beating up on you?"

"Didn't you hear me, Sterling? I don't want to talk about it." Her voice was strained almost to breaking point.

The eyes that swept her face were far too perceptive. "An assault of some sort?"

She should have known he would guess, although even Sterling could not guess all of it. She tried to head him off. "Now look, Sterling—"

"Am I right? Is that what it was?"

"I keep telling you, it was a dream! Don't you ever have nightmares, Sterling?" He nodded. "Then stop harassing me."

"Questions aren't harassment."

"It's over now, that's all that matters. Please go, Sterling."

He shrugged. "If you say so."

He was moving away from the bed when she said, "I never asked—why did you come into the house?"

"I was out with the dogs. We usually go for a bit of a run before I turn in. I heard you screaming, and I knew I had to help."

"It won't happen again," Sara told him flatly. "You're

my boss, Sterling. All the same, I will not have you coming in here without permission. Especially when I'm asleep.''

A hard look came into the rugged face. "Don't even try to suggest I took advantage of you."

"Didn't you? Sitting on my bed. Holding me." Sara's voice shook. "Stroking me."

"Comforting you," Sterling corrected.

"Don't tell me you didn't enjoy it."

"Actually, I enjoyed it very much," he drawled.

Sara was angry suddenly. Angry at Sterling, angry at herself for having been excited by his closeness, angry at the vital sexuality she sensed every time she was near him.

"I've told you how I feel about being touched."

"More than a few times," he said sarcastically. "If it's any comfort to you, Sara, you may as well know—I never force my attentions on unwilling women."

Women... Were there women in Sterling's life? He was not married, but was there one woman in particular? It made no sense that the answer mattered so much.

CHAPTER FOUR

As SARA bent over one of the drawers of the filing cabinet, the sun shafting through the windows caught the glossy fair hair and gilded it with streaks of gold. Her forehead was puckered with concentration as she riffled through folders before depositing the one in her hand.

In the open doorway, Sterling stood very still watching the graceful figure. She was incredibly slender, yet at the same time her appearance had an almost contradictory suggestion of ripening femininity. It was a quality Sterling registered without being able to explain it to himself.

She dropped the folder in its appropriate place and walked to the desk. So far she hadn't seen him. He knew he should call attention to himself—already he knew Sara well enough to sense that she would hate to be watched without knowing it—but the sight of her was affording him such pleasure that he was loath to break the moment.

Sara had been at the estate almost forty-eight hours, and he was as captivated by her now as he had been the first time he'd set eyes on her in the diner. Maybe more so. She was the loveliest girl he had ever known.

Time and again, he had to restrain himself from pulling her into his arms. He longed to kiss her, to stroke the smooth hair, to cover her with caresses.

He wondered how she would look unclothed. It was a thought that made him smile wryly. Sara would have a fit if she knew how badly he wanted to make love to her.

More than anything, he longed to know her better. He wanted to know why the thought of a man's touch brought the haunted expression to her eyes and why she was so frightened of anything that even hinted of sex.

He wanted to be the man who would remove that fear and awaken her to womanhood.

"Sara," he said softly.

She spun. "Sterling! I didn't hear you come in."

He saw she was pale, and beneath her eyes were dark smudges. Sterling had to restrain himself from touching them.

He grinned at her. "That's because you were so absorbed in your work."

"I haven't done very much yet. Just a bit of filing."

"All you can do, really, till I give you some correspondence."

"Is that why you're here, Sterling? You're going to dictate?" She reached for a steno pad and a pencil.

"No, it's something else."

"Oh?" she asked warily.

Would he ever learn the reason for her wariness?

Easily, he said, "Time I gave you a tour of the vineyards."

In an instant, she relaxed. "Oh, yes, I'd like that!"

As she smiled, Sterling drew in his breath. With the haunted look gone, color came into her face, and her eyes shone like jewels. God, but she was lovely when she gave herself a chance!

She laughed when she saw the conveyance he used to make his way through the lands, an all-terrain vehicle painted bright scarlet and open at the front and sides.

"Reminds me of a motorized cart I used to ride at the zoo when I was a kid."

"Not much different," he agreed, laughing with her.

He drove slowly along the paths that wound through the rolling land of the vineyards. Occasionally, he cast a glance at Sara, gratified to see how eagerly she looked from side to side. She asked many questions, intelligent ones, about the grapes—how they were planted, when they were harvested, the wines into which they were made. She loved the view of the hills, with the colored air balloons floating above them, and wanted to know whether there were hiking paths.

"It's a wonderful place," she said, when they turned back at last.

"I agree. But it's my home, so perhaps I'm prejudiced."

"You're not prejudiced," Sara said.

Something made him want to ask whether she could see herself living here permanently, but he bit back the question the moment it entered his mind. For one thing, it would bring the frightened look to her eyes. For another, it made no sense that he would even want to ask the question. Sara was gorgeous, but she was also unusual, and as yet he knew so little about her.

None of which seemed to matter very much, because he knew that he was fast falling in love with her.

On a high, hilly slope he stopped, and they got out of the open car. It was a beautiful summer day, the sky blue and cloudless. Below them spread the valley, a golden quilt of terraces and vines.

"I keep thinking it can't get any better, and then it does," she said, her eyes on the view.

"No views where you come from?"

Her eyes sparkled as she looked at him. "Magnificent, but different."

"Where *are* you from, Sara?"

"It isn't important. And if you think you can trap me, you can't."

"Just thought I'd try," he teased, playing along with her.

They left the hill and Sterling took a different route, one that ran along a creek. He stopped not far from the water and drew out a basket from behind one of the rear seats.

"Picnic time," he explained.

"Do you do this often?" Sara seemed intrigued.

"As often as I can. Best way to eat is out-of-doors. Especially in the company of a beautiful woman."

He was surprised when her eyes left his. But a second later she was looking at him. "Sounds great," she said brightly.

He spread a rug over the ground, sat near its center and motioned Sara to sit, too. She hesitated before squatting on the rug's farthest corner. Like an animal aware of possible danger, Sterling thought, wondering again why she was so frightened.

He unpacked a French loaf, fat cherry tomatoes and a wedge of Camembert cheese, then took out a bottle of wine and two glasses.

"Wow!" Sara said.

"Meaning you're aghast or impressed?"

"Impressed!"

"And you'll eat for a change?"

"How can I not?"

She ate more than Sterling expected. But when he wanted to pour her some wine, she stopped him.

"Not even a little?" he asked.

She hesitated. "No, thanks."

Somehow they got talking about music, and in no time at all they were discussing a band that was enjoying increasing popularity all over the country. It turned out that Sara knew a few of the songs off by heart. With little prompting, she began to sing, and Sterling hummed along because he knew the music but not the words.

From there they went to other topics, and Sterling was amazed to see how naturally Sara laughed and talked. In fact, he couldn't remember the last time he had enjoyed a woman's company quite so much.

He dropped a piece of bread on the rug, and before he could pick it up, a bird swooped and took it.

"Cheeky," Sara said. When a second bird descended on the first and grabbed the morsel from its beak, she burst out laughing. "There you are, bird, that will teach you what it feels like!"

Sterling was enchanted not by the interplay of the birds but with the spontaneity of Sara's amusement.

"Did you see that, Sterling?"

Her eyes shone with laughter. This was not the woman who had sobbed last night in the throes of some dreadful nightmare.

"What I see," Sterling said softly, "is the real Sara."

She looked at him, amusement still in her face. "What on earth do you mean?"

"The woman with a sense of humor and a zest for life. I knew there had to be something positive lurking behind the sad expression and the haunted eyes."

"Lordy, Sterling, you're dramatic!"

"You intrigue me, Sara. You have from the moment I set eyes on you."

"You mean the moment you quit my job for me."

"Actually," he said deliberately, "you intrigued me days before that. Why do you think I kept coming back to the diner?"

She looked startled. "Are you saying you came because of me?"

"You're very unusual, Sara."

Suddenly the wary look was in her eyes. "What you see is what I am. I'm really very ordinary."

"You're not ordinary at all."

She cut off a sliver of Camembert and spread it over a piece of French bread. Her hands, Sterling noticed, were not quite steady.

A question hovered on his lips. Was this the right time to ask it? Would the time ever be right?

Quietly, he said, "Sara—who is Larry?"

She jerked backward as fiercely as if she had been burned. In a second, the color had drained from her cheeks.

"Larry?" Her voice shook.

"That's right. Who is he?" Sterling's calm tone belied a nonchalance he was far from feeling.

"Why...why do you ask?"

"Larry was the name you were crying out last night."

"When I had the nightmare?"

"That's right."

This time it was Sara's turn to drop some bread. Neither of them noticed the bird that swooped down on it. Sara sprang to her feet, knocking down Sterling's wineglass as she moved. She was trembling so violently that he wondered if she was going to faint.

A wave of compassion swept him. This lovely girl was in the grip of something terrible. He longed to hold her, to cradle the fragile body, to tell her he would never let anything hurt her.

Clearly, mention of Larry had upset her. It would be so easy to leave the subject alone. But now, more than ever, he knew he had to continue.

"Who is he, Sara?"

"Why does he have to be anybody?" Her voice was so tight, it sounded as if it was about to crack. "Don't you dream, Sterling?"

"Sure I do."

"Do you remember your dreams?" she demanded. "Do the things you dream make sense?"

"Most of the time it's all one big mix-up," he conceded.

"Then why press me about my dream?"

She was so distressed, perhaps he should just leave it. Sara was right, after all. A minute after waking he was hardly ever able to remember even the slightest details of a dream. He seldom had nightmares, and even then, a lingering memory was often all that remained—along with relief that what had made his heart pound had in fact never happened.

Yet for some reason he could not leave this. There had been a lot more to Sara's nightmare than she wanted him to believe. The intensity of her reaction to his questions told him that.

"You were so definite," he said slowly.

"I couldn't have been." She was ashen.

"This guy, Larry. He wasn't some nebulous person,

someone you don't know. You were terribly upset, Sara. Even after I woke you, you were sobbing.''

"Oh, God!" She pushed a fevered hand through her hair. "I wish you'd stop!"

"Did he do something bad, this Larry?"

"Stop!" Her voice had risen.

"Did he try to kiss you?" A thought struck him. "He didn't try to rape you?" he asked, appalled.

"This is ridiculous!" Sara shouted. "Okay, so I once knew a Larry. For some reason, I dreamed about him. Can't you leave it at that?"

"No."

Bitterly, she turned on him. "This outing was a trap. I should have known."

"What are you talking about?"

"You lured me here deliberately."

"That's nonsense, Sara."

"I know about men like you, Sterling."

"Are you saying I'm like Larry?"

Her eyes were bright with anger. "Leave Larry out of this. He has nothing to do with it. It's you we're talking about. Oh, you were so clever, weren't you, Sterling? Bringing me on a tour of your beautiful vineyards. A picnic. Catching me off my guard. And all the while, you were waiting to attack."

"I just asked you one very simple question."

"To which I gave you an answer. If you don't accept it, that's your problem, Sterling."

"I wonder."

After a long moment, Sara said, "What if there really is someone called Larry?"

"It would prove my point."

"What point, Sterling?" She paused, then said, "Okay, so there is a Larry. Satisfied?"

"I knew it."

"A person I once knew. In the past. Of no relevance to my present life."

A pulse was beating hard in the side of her neck. She

was more agitated than Sterling had ever seen her. He knew it was time to give her a break, to let her calm down. But there were still things he had to know. And if he didn't ask them now, he might never get the answers he needed.

"Just two things," he said.

"Not even one," she replied furiously. "I'm going back to the office."

Sterling caught up with her as she was walking away. "I'll drive you back."

"It isn't necessary."

"I'll drive you all the same." He hated to go on, but he sensed that he had to. "Are you married, Sara?"

"Of course not!" she said scornfully.

"Have you ever been?"

"No."

The answer made him quite extraordinarily happy, which was amazing. Sterling, who was never short of a woman if he wanted a date, had never given serious thought to marriage before. He didn't even know if he was thinking that way now.

"This Larry... Does he have anything to do with your fear of being touched?"

"You're making a big deal out of nothing," she snapped. "I have a meaningless nightmare and I call out a name. And that's enough for you to go drawing conclusions."

If only he knew why she was so tense. "I'm only trying to understand, Sara."

"People have nightmares all the time. They don't have to mean anything. What are you anyway, Sterling Tayler? An amateur psychologist?"

"A man who's concerned about you," he said slowly.

"I don't need your concern! I don't want it!" Brave words, but her voice shook.

He couldn't press her. Quietly he said, "Get in the car, Sara, and I'll drive you back."

"No more questions about Larry."

"Okay," he said pleasantly, and added to himself, *At least not today.*

They were both silent on the way through the vineyards. Out of the corner of his eye, Sterling could see that Sara's hands were curled in her lap so tightly the knuckles were white.

Who is Larry? he wondered. *And how do I get to know Sara better? How do I get close to her?*

Sara lifted her head at the sound of a car outside her office. She went to the window in time to see Sterling's car disappearing around the corner. He was on his way to town to pick up a fresh supply of wine labels. She knew it because he had mentioned the fact in the course of dictation earlier.

Two days had passed since the picnic in the vineyards. Yesterday a tour group had come to the estate. Sterling had led the group through the wineries, and Sara had joined it, listening to the things Sterling said about wine making. Other than the tour and the dictation, there had been no contact between them.

Listlessly, she went to her desk, put her fingers on the keyboard and looked at her notes. She typed a few words, then stopped, stood once more and began to pace the office.

Something of Sterling's earthy male smell still lingered on the air. Imagination, of course! But there it was. Try as she would, she could not seem to lose the erotic scent of him in her nostrils. Just as she could not rid herself of the longing that sprang from somewhere deep inside her and spread to the rest of her body.

This would never do! It must be the heat that was getting to her. On the way to the office she had made a detour via the swimming pool. Each time she saw the pool she longed to dive into it. She knew why she hadn't done so, of course. She didn't want Sterling to see her in a swimsuit.

But Sterling would be away for some time, two hours at the very least. It was safe to swim now.

It didn't take her long to go to her room and change out of her clothes. A few minutes later, she was diving into the pool. The water was cool and lovely, just as she'd known it would be. She swam four lengths, then turned on her back, closed her eyes and floated.

Bliss, she thought, as the sun warmed her wet body and the water moved gently beneath her. This was as close to heaven as a person could get. Closer than she had been in a long while.

She couldn't have said when she had the sense that she was being watched. Her eyes snapped open, and there was Sterling, kneeling at the side of the pool. Sara dropped her feet to the ground in an instant.

"Didn't mean to disturb you." His eyes sparkled with devilment.

"How long have you been there?" She spoke in a low voice to hide her distress.

"Not long at all."

"You shouldn't be here, Sterling."

His eyebrows lifted. "An indictment, Sara?"

"You were going into town."

"I did say that," he agreed lazily.

He was enjoying this. Hateful man! But then, weren't they all? Not one of them that you could trust.

"You couldn't have driven there and back so quickly."

"Actually," Sterling drawled, "I hadn't gone more than a few miles when I realized I'd left my wallet behind and came back for it."

"And on your way to the house you just happened to see me in the pool."

"That's right. Anything wrong with that?"

"You misled me on purpose," she accused. "You knew you'd be back. That you'd catch me."

"Are you kidding, Sara? How could I possibly know you'd go swimming the moment my back was turned?"

"You couldn't," she conceded after a moment. "But I believe you hoped to catch me in *some* act."

"Not that it matters. You can use the pool any time you like."

"As long as it's not during working time," she muttered.

"Wouldn't bother me if it was. You're the conscientious sort, Sara. I know you'll always find time for your work."

His eyes were going over her, moving from her wet hair and face down her throat and arms over her breasts. Sara was trembling as she lowered herself in the water, where he wouldn't see more than her head.

Sterling grinned at her. "Are you really so modest, Sara?"

"I don't like being watched." Despite the effort to speak firmly, her voice shook. "And you were watching me, Sterling."

"Can you blame me?"

"Yes! You should have said something right away. Why didn't you?"

"Has it occurred to you that you're a treat for male eyes?"

The water had lost its magic. "I wish you wouldn't say things like that," she said unhappily.

"You're a very beautiful woman, Sara."

"Sterling... Sterling, don't."

"Does it bother you so much that I find you attractive?"

I love being beautiful in your eyes. The words appeared involuntarily in her mind. *Oh, God, what's happening to me? How could I even think such an appalling thing?*

"I just don't like it when you talk that way," she said in a low voice.

"Why not, Sara?"

"The things you say... It's all man talk."

"Actually," Sterling said, "they're not unusual things

for a man to say to a very lovely woman. But perhaps you
don't know that.''

''Should I?''

''Did Larry ever say things like that to you, Sara?''

''You're fixated on this Larry, Sterling. Just because I
mentioned a man's name in a dream, it doesn't mean anything. I wish you'd forget about him.'' She tried unsuccessfully to keep the quiver from her voice.

Slowly, Sterling said, ''Maybe there hasn't been a man
in your life. There's something so innocent about you,
Sara. So untouched.''

She couldn't meet his eyes. ''What do you mean?''

''The way you look, the way you behave. It's as if
you've never experienced sex of any kind. Am I right,
Sara?''

Still she couldn't meet the male gaze that was making
her shiver at the same time as she was angered by it. In
a nearby tree, two birds were conducting a loud, squawk-
ing argument. After a second, one bird flew away with a
noisy fluttering of wings. If only she had the freedom to
get away with such ease, Sara thought longingly.

''Am I right?'' Sterling asked again.

She didn't owe him an explanation. But Sterling had
the look of a man who wouldn't leave without one.

She looked at him. ''You know how I feel about touching, about kissing,'' she said in a low voice.

''Meaning you're a virgin.''

Would he never stop?

''I can't tell you more than that I'm not interested in
sex,'' she told him flatly. ''That should answer all your
questions, Sterling.''

The eyes that searched her face were very dark, very
attractive in their frame of long lashes. The sun shining
on his face emphasized the whiteness of his teeth and the
tautness of his tanned skin. He was the most striking man
she had ever set eyes on.

A wave of longing swept Sara suddenly, fierce and un-
trammeled. Treacherously came the question—what

would it be like to make love with this man? Without thinking, she moved toward him.

A second later, she stared at him, appalled. She was no longer thinking rationally as she stood up straight. There was only the need to get out of the water, to remove herself from danger. Quickly.

"Sara!"

The horror in his voice caught her. "Yes?"

"That mark. On your arm. What is it?"

Her eyes followed the direction of his. In a second, she realized what he was staring at. In one of his fits of temper, Larry had lunged at her with a piece of jagged glass. All the other bruises he had caused had faded, but the damage done by the broken glass had left an ugly scar.

Sterling hadn't noticed the scar until now because her arms had been submerged in water. When she was dressed, the scar was always hidden by a sleeve. It was only in her hurry to get away from him that she had stood up straight in the pool.

"What is it, Sara?"

"Just a little scar." She tried to sound offhand.

"Just must have hurt yourself badly. What happened?"

He was determined not to be fobbed off. And she was equally determined not to tell him the facts. And if that was lying, the lie was justified, because Larry and the things he had done to her were none of Sterling's business.

"An accident," she said, as nonchalantly as she could.

"Must have been a hell of an accident. I can't imagine what could cause a scar like that."

"A piece of broken glass," she told him.

"You fell on glass?" And when she didn't answer immediately, he said, "Must have been quite an impact."

Even now, months later, Sara could still remember the awful searing pain she had felt when Larry had attacked her. She remembered her fear, a fear that was more terrible than physical pain. "Quite an impact," she agreed, her mouth dry.

"My poor Sara."

There was a note in his voice that unnerved her. For a moment she could only stare at him numbly. "I'm not *your* Sara," she whispered when she could speak.

"We'll see about that."

The breath stuck in Sara's throat as Sterling stripped out of his T-shirt and jeans. For a long moment he stood poised above her, clad only in a pair of white Jockey shorts, a tall, tanned figure, lean yet muscular, more beautiful than a marble sculpture, infinitely more powerful.

He dove, cleaving the water with barely a splash. It all happened so quickly that Sara barely had time to think. By the time she was scrambling for the edge of the pool, he was beside her.

"My poor Sara," he said again.

With his wet hair and face, he looked even sexier than before. Water clung to his throat and shoulders like a thousand small teardrops, making Sara long to kiss them away.

But she had to get away from him. Strange how that thought always came to her just a second too late.

She was heaving herself out of the pool when a pair of strong hands gripped her waist and pulled her into the water.

"Don't!" The word emerged as a sob.

"I'm not going to hurt you," he said softly.

Before she could stop him, he bent his head and brushed the scar with his lips. Once up and down, the touch feather light and madly arousing.

Sara stifled a gasp as fire shot through her. She hadn't expected this, hadn't guessed it was coming. It was all she could do to stop herself from arching toward Sterling.

Somehow—heaven only knew where she found the strength—she managed to meet his eyes when he straightened and looked at her.

"I wish I could do something to erase the scar," he said softly.

"It will always be there."

"Children have their hurts taken away by kisses."

She was regaining a small measure of control. "I'm not a child, Sterling."

"You aren't," he agreed, and his eyes traveled over her once more, sensuously yet also thoughtfully. "You're all woman, Sara. A very beautiful woman."

"I keep telling you not to say things like that!"

"I'll say more." Wicked fingers slid erotically up her neck, lingering on the small hollow where her pulse was beating a riotous tattoo.

Aware of the powerful and very urgent needs of her body, she stared despairingly at Sterling. He was so close to her, his bare torso tanned and muscular and glistening with water, his legs too excitingly close to hers. The passion she had thought long dead was rising inside her, weakening her limbs, threatening to overwhelm her.

Sterling kissed her again. This time the lips on her arm were firmer, sexier, the path they took more deliberate. The tip of a strong tongue on Sara's scar almost drove her out of her mind.

She wasn't thinking as her hands went to his head and her fingers buried themselves in the thick dark hair and tried to bring him closer to her. It was a second or two before the realization of what she was doing made its impact, and then her pulling became an urgent pushing. She pushed as hard as she could, telling herself—*wishing*—that Sterling would take her behavior as proof of her revulsion.

But when the damp, dark-haired head lifted, the eyes that met hers were so deep with knowledge that Sara shivered.

"Did I tell you that you're desirable?" he asked roughly.

Painfully, she shook her head. "You said...you said..."

"What did I say, Sara?"

"That I was beautiful."

"More than that. Far more than that."

Reality returned, and with it a dreadful sense of danger. "I don't want to hear this!"

"Desirable, Sara. Beautiful. Sexy beyond belief."

"Don't you understand?" she shouted. "What does it take to get through to you, Sterling?"

"To get through to *you*," he countered softly.

"Me?"

"To show you what life is about. What you're about. To show you the real Sara. The passionate Sara who needs to be kissed. Often."

The words stunned her. She was momentarily unable to speak. Later, she would think up a clever answer, but now, with the dark eyes holding hers and the blood throbbing in her veins, rational thought was impossible.

"If I can't kiss the scar away, I'll kiss away the memory of what caused it."

With those words, Sterling bent his head once more. Only this time, instead of kissing Sara's arm, his lips found her mouth.

The shock of the contact was so intense that Sara reared, startled as a skittish horse. Sterling groaned. Then he pulled her against him, one arm firmly around her waist, the other supporting the back of her neck.

Once more, his lips found hers, his kisses deep, passionate, searching. Sara did not fight him. She could no more fight him at this moment than she could stop breathing, not when the taste of his lips gave her such intense pleasure. He was much taller than she was, so that her feet were inches above the floor of the pool, and he held her body so tightly against his that she could feel the evidence of his passion and desire throbbing against her.

The moment came when Sara could no longer restrain her passion. With Sterling exploring her lips, teasing them with his tongue, she opened her mouth to him. One kiss followed another, sweet kisses, drugging, a mutual exploration that encompassed lips and mouths and also bodies. Mindlessly, thoughtlessly, Sara gave herself over to the pleasure and passion of the moment.

Sanity returned only when Sterling stopped kissing her so he could slide the straps of her swimsuit from her shoulders. As his fingers touched Sara's breasts, she pushed backward, her feet paddling rapidly inches above the pool bottom.

"No!" she gasped.

"But, Sara, you—"

"Don't say it!" She was horrified. "Whatever it is, don't say it!"

"I don't understand."

He was reaching for her again, but she was thinking clearly and was ready for him. Though she wanted, quite desperately, to go into his arms, she understood how close she had come to the point of no stopping. Shock at what had so nearly happened gave her the strength to get away from him.

"Sara, please."

"No!" she shouted.

A few quick strokes took her to the edge of the pool. She was about to climb out when Sterling caught up with her.

"Why?" he asked, making no effort to touch her.

"Why?" She threw the word back at him.

"Why did you stop?"

"The question, Sterling, is why did you start?" she countered flatly.

She couldn't control her trembling. She could only hope that Sterling would put the tremors down to her being cold rather than to what they really were—the product of un-requited desire.

"Don't you understand, Sara?" His breath was warm against her wet throat. "I know how innocent you are. But surely you must know that no man could look at you without wanting to kiss you. I can't imagine why it hasn't happened to you before now." His voice was rough, yet tender, too.

The unexpected tenderness coming from this tough and powerful man was almost Sara's undoing. She had grown used to harshness. Tenderness undermined her defenses, making her vulnerable. Sterling had to be stopped before he lured her into a situation that was impossible to escape or resist.

"You know how much I hate the thought of sex." She made her voice deliberately hard as she fell back on the only excuse she could give him. "And yet you forced yourself on me all the same."

"There was no force, Sara. At no time was there force."

It was difficult to contradict him when what he was saying was true. "You knew I didn't want it." Her lips trembled. "You didn't ask for permission."

"Do you really think people ask for permission before kissing?" His voice was at her throat.

"I don't know what…what people do. I just know that I…I want to be asked before someone touches me."

"That's silly, Sara."

"It may be to you," she said heatedly, unsuccessfully trying to twist away from him. "It may be silly to other people. But other people don't concern me, Sterling. I can only tell you what is right for me."

"I see."

He was standing so close beside her it was difficult to leave the pool. "If you'll move," she said, "I want to get out of the water."

After a long moment, Sterling stood aside. Uncertain whether she was relieved or disappointed—and wasn't *that* insane!—Sara climbed out of the pool.

She was about to walk away when he called to her. "Sara."

She turned and looked at him. Waist-deep in water, his chest dark and rippling with muscle, his expression dangerous, he looked like some pagan god ascending from an ancient lake.

"Yes?"

"I can't help wondering—do you actually believe the things you say?"

Sara stiffened. "What do you mean?"

"Are you so sure you hate sex?"

"I keep telling you I do!"

"I know what you tell me. I also know—" his voice deepened "—that for quite a time you seemed to be enjoying our kisses."

Sara grew rigid. "You don't know what you're talking about."

"Don't I? There were things I didn't imagine, Sara. Your hands in my hair. Your lips opening to mine. The way you arched your back. Interesting behavior for someone who claims she's not interested in sex."

Sara felt a fiery heat staining her cheeks, but she was powerless to do anything about it. "You are despicable," she said very clearly.

"Because I point out certain undeniable facts?"

"Undeniable in your revolting male mind, Sterling Tayler."

"This isn't an argument, Sara. I'm just telling you that you seemed to be enjoying what happened."

"I *hated* it. I—" Sara stopped. Sterling was right, of course. There were facts that could not be denied. She put her hands to her hot cheeks, wishing she could hide the flush.

"Maybe…maybe I was swept along," she conceded at last.

"Then you *did* feel something."

If Sterling had even the least inkling of how much she had felt—the wild beating of her heart, the throbbing in her veins, the clamorings of her body—he would not rest until he got her to sleep with him. And however much she might want it—no denying that there had been a few moments when she really had wanted to make love with him—she would never sleep with Sterling. She would not sleep with any man.

"I can only tell you what I feel right now," she said succinctly. "Contempt. Disdain. Nothing else, Sterling."

The lids came down over his eyes, and in the strong

jaw something moved. "But you did feel something, Sara," he persisted.

"If I did, *if,* Sterling, then the feeling vanished very quickly. I want you to forget this ever happened."

"Impossible, Sara."

"If you don't—" she paused "—I'll have to leave."

A few seconds passed. Sterling stood in the pool, the water eddying around him. Tensely, barely breathing, Sara waited for his answer. The words she had spoken had been foolhardy rather than brave, for she didn't want to leave the estate. Not now, not yet. Yet she also knew that unless Sterling undertook to leave her alone, she could not stay here.

"I can't forget," he said at last.

"I'll go and pack," she said dully over the sudden pain in her chest.

"Not so fast. You gave me a commitment, Sara."

"That's right," she conceded dully.

"A verbal one, true, but I trusted you when you gave it. You can't go back on it now."

"Sterling…"

He held up a hand. "I haven't finished. I said I couldn't forget what happened. What I can try and do is not refer to it. At least for the moment."

"Never," Sara said.

"For the moment," Sterling repeated.

And with that, Sara knew, she had to be satisfied. It was as much of a concession as she was likely to get from Sterling.

CHAPTER FIVE

"YOU'VE been avoiding me for two days now."

Pulse quickening, Sara looked up from her desk. "I've been busy."

"Not so busy."

"Busy enough," she said shortly.

"We won't argue about it, but I do want to know the reason."

"Does there have to be a reason, Sterling?"

"You know there does," he mocked. "You've been taking great care to keep out of my way, and don't tell me I've been imagining it, because we both know I haven't. So what is it, Sara?"

She shifted restlessly beneath the intensity of the dark-eyed gaze. "You're not going to give up, are you?" Her eyes were troubled.

"Of course not." Sterling paused, then went on laconically, "Still bothered by those kisses?"

Sara jerked. "You mean the ones in the pool?"

"Were there others?" There was a touch of laughter in his voice.

She looked away from him. "I don't think about them."

"And I think," Sterling said, taking a step toward her, "that you're not telling the truth."

"They were just kisses, for heaven's sake!"

"I agree—that's all they were."

Tensely, Sara said, "Having established that, can we change the subject?"

"When you've heard me out. I'm here to tell you that you don't need to be scared of me."

"Give me a break, Sterling!"

"When you're ready to kiss me, you will."

"It will never happen!" Sara declared angrily.

Sterling laughed softly. "Remembering your response in the pool, I think you're mistaken."

At his tone, Sara lifted her chin. "We've already talked about what went on in the pool. For some reason—heaven only knows why—I lost my head. I don't know why it happened. It won't happen again. And if you weren't my employer, I'd call you a bastard for bringing it up."

"You've just found a rather neat way of calling me that anyway." He didn't sound at all perturbed. "Stop avoiding me, Sara. I won't press you to do anything that makes you uncomfortable."

"Fine," she muttered.

"That being the case, don't run the other way whenever you see me coming. And stop looking so indignant. I've seen you do it." Once more there was that hint of laughter. "There are so few of us on the estate, you can't stay out of my way forever."

Involuntarily, her lips tilted at the corners. "You've made your point, no need to go on about it."

"Hey!" Sterling exclaimed. "Do I see a smile?"

He was smiling, too, the extraordinary smile that shafted its way straight to her heart whenever she saw it.

"Perhaps a very little smile," she conceded.

"A very little smile is better than no smile. Especially when it's so beautiful."

"Are you flirting with me, Sterling Tayler?" Sara was unable to prevent the sparkle that came to her eyes.

"Is that what I'm doing?"

"As if you didn't know! You're a smooth one, Sterling. You tell me you won't kiss me and then you flirt with me, instead."

"Do you have anything against flirtatious men, Sara?"

She thought of Larry and the way he had flirted and flattered her into his life and his bed. "I can't bear the sight of them," she said abruptly.

"In that case, I won't flirt with you again."

But as he forced the corners of his lips downward, he looked so comical that Sara couldn't help laughing.

Briefly, she saw something flash in the dark eyes, and she caught her breath.

"If only you weren't so irresistible," he said in a tone that made her senses leap.

"You're still flirting."

"Just telling you that one day you *will* want to kiss me. Sooner or later, the time will be right."

"I doubt that, Sterling." She wished she could control her breathing, which was way too fast.

If only Sterling wasn't so dynamic. Deep inside, Sara felt a gnawing, a sensation that was part longing, part pain. Despite all her bravado, despite her terrible experiences with Larry, there was something she wanted from Sterling, only it was more than he could ever give her. It seemed that she could rationalize all she wanted, but the longing never went away. All it did was grow stronger.

"Nearly forgot," he said, "I'm here to talk about something else, as well. A tour group is arriving tomorrow."

Her eyes lit with interest. "And you want me to follow you around again?"

Sterling grinned. "Actually, I want you to lead this tour yourself."

She was startled. "I hope I'm ready for it."

"Have to start sometime. Why not give it a try, Sara? I think you can do it."

"Thanks for the confidence, but I'm not sure I know enough about wine making."

"You've had a tour and listened to me talk, and I'll give you some extra stuff to read." He slanted her a quizzical look. "Well, Sara? Will you try it?"

She hesitated before saying, "Yes."

"Excellent." Sterling looked satisfied. "I suggest another quick private tour now so you can ask me anything you're not certain about. You'll be all set by tomorrow."

Excitement gripped Sara as she explored the wineries with Sterling. On this, her third visit, the dark cellars, the

How to play

and claim as many as
FIVE FREE GIFTS:

1. With a coin, carefully scratch away the silver boxes opposite. Then check the Super Bingo Claim Chart to see how many FREE GIFTS you can claim.

2. Send back this card and you'll receive specially selected Mills & Boon® romances from the Enchanted™ series. These books are yours to keep absolutely FREE.

3. There's no catch. You're under no obligation to buy anything. We charge you nothing for your first shipment. And you don't have to make a minimum number of purchases - not even one!

4. The fact is, thousands of readers enjoy receiving books by mail from the Reader Service™. They like the convenience of home delivery and they like getting the best new romance novels at least a month before they are available in the shops. And of course postage and packing is completely FREE!

5. We hope that after receiving your free books you'll want to remain a subscriber. But the choice is yours - to continue or cancel, anytime at all! So why not accept our no risk invitation. You'll be glad you did!

YOURS FREE WHEN YOU MATCH 5 NUMBERS!

We all love mysteries… so as well as your free books, there may also be an intriguing gift waiting for you! Simply scratch away the silver boxes and check the claim chart to see what you can receive.

Play

SUPER BINGO !....

Scratch away the silver boxes above to reveal your five lucky numbers and see how many match your bingo card. Then simply check the claim chart below to see how many FREE gifts we have for you!

SUPER BINGO CLAIM CHART	
Match 5 numbers	**WORTH 4 FREE BOOKS** **PLUS A MYSTERY GIFT**
Match 4 numbers	**WORTH 4 FREE BOOKS**
Match 3 numbers	**WORTH 3 FREE BOOKS**

YES! I have scratched off the silver boxes above. Please send me all the gifts for which I qualify. I understand that I am under no obligation to purchase any books, as explained on the opposite page. I am over 18 years of age.

MS/MRS/MISS/MR   INITIALS   N9DI

                                                       BLOCK CAPITALS PLEASE

SURNAME

ADDRESS

POSTCODE

NO STAMP NEEDED!

THE READER SERVICE™
FREEPOST CN81
CROYDON
SURREY
CR9 3WZ

If offer card is missing, write to: The Reader Service, P.O. Box 236, Croydon, Surrey CR9 3RU.

NO
STAMP
NEEDED IF
POSTED IN
THE U.K.
OR N. I.

big barrels, the strong fermentation smells were beginning to be familiar.

"What do you think?" Sterling asked.

"I can probably cope."

What was much harder to cope with were the feelings that rushed at her when they walked together. As they made their way through the narrow space between two rows of oak barrels, Sara was unaware that she had closed the distance between herself and Sterling. It was only when a hard thigh brushed against her that she realized how close they were to each other.

As Sterling turned toward her in the semidarkness, Sara's breath caught in her throat. The longing to go into his arms was almost overwhelming. Abruptly, she stepped away from him, but not before she heard his low laugh.

"So you can cope?" he asked when they emerged into the sunlight.

"Yes." The answer came a second too late.

"Glad to hear it."

Sterling laughed again, and Sara knew they had not been talking about the wineries.

When he asked her to have dinner with him, her refusal came too quickly. She wanted quite desperately to say yes and knew it would be a mistake.

"If I'm going to lead a tour tomorrow, I've a lot of reading to do tonight, Sterling."

"Another time then," he said casually, and the words seemed to hold a promise of a kind.

When the group arrived at noon the next day, Sara was ready.

Besides the wealth of information she had gleaned from Sterling, she had spent hours the previous night reading about wine making. She knew all about the grapes that were grown on the estate and the wines that were made there. She could answer questions about every step of the wine-making process.

"Aren't you diligent," Sterling teased her the next

morning. "Saw your light still on when I went walking at midnight."

Sara smiled at him. "Nothing like being prepared. I don't want to disgrace you."

"You could never do that." Sterling's gaze swept her face in a way that set her pulse racing.

She knew she should leave it at that, yet she couldn't help asking, "How can you be so certain?"

"There are things a man knows."

He was studying her, his eyes traveling slowly from her face to the pulse that beat too quickly in the hollow of her throat. Controlling a sudden shiver, Sara looked away from him.

When she saw the bus coming down the drive, she went out to meet it. She had dressed in her good brown pants, which she was still able to fasten, and a cream-colored silk shirt. Her hair was swept back, and long gold hoops adorned her ears. Sterling's very male look of approval gave her a jolt of pleasure as well as a boost of confidence.

The bus stopped beside the wineries, and the guide jumped out. Introducing himself as Mike, he gave Sara a look that was not very different from Sterling's. He shook her hand, told her he was glad she was going to be conducting the tour, and by then people were starting to get off the bus.

As Sara prepared to welcome them, she noticed Sterling walking away from the wineries. She had thought he would walk along and evaluate her performance and was relieved that he had the tact and the confidence to let her handle this alone.

There were about twenty people in the group, mainly from the eastern states, touring California and stopping at points of interest along the way. A few casual questions elicited the information that for most of them this was the first visit to the Napa Valley.

Sara was about to begin her talk before leading the group into the wineries when a man, identified by his name tag as Albert, touched her arm. "Haven't we met?"

She flinched instinctively at the physical contact. But since the question was casual enough, she kept her tone friendly. "Not that I know of."

"Your face is familiar," Albert persisted.

A big, florid-faced fellow in a brightly flowered shirt with a camera and a camcorder dangling around his neck, he reminded Sara of Larry's father, a supremely arrogant man who thought his only son was a gift to any woman. Sara had never told Larry's parents that he was blackmailing and abusing her. For one thing, they wouldn't have believed her. For another, they'd have taken her story straight to Larry, who would have made her pay for her crime with his fists.

She saw Mike shoot her a quick glance as she said sharply, "I'm quite sure we've never met."

"And I *know* we have."

Sara took a breath, then started the talk she had prepared, careful to make eye contact with the group as she spoke. Yet always, on the periphery of her vision, there was Albert.

Though she tried to concentrate on what she was saying, all the time she was wondering. Was Albert right? Had they met? His face was unfamiliar, but she supposed it was possible she had run into him somewhere.

Mike must have sensed the tension she was trying to hide, for as they began to walk toward the wineries—Albert just inches from her—Mike drew her away from the group.

"Keep it cool," he warned in an undertone. "Don't let the guy get to you."

"Easier said than done. He's stalking me—or haven't you noticed?"

"I wouldn't call it stalking." Mike sounded impatient.

"Wherever I go, there he is."

"So he's a creep. There's one on every tour."

"I don't have to put up with it."

"Wrong, Sara. I get paid to lead tours, your boss gets paid to let us on to his property. We're in business, Sara.

Like it or not, we have to act professionally. Granted, the guy bugs you, but you can't let him affect you. At least not so anyone can notice.''

Mike was right, Sara knew. As she struggled for composure, she was glad she had made a point of familiarizing herself with all the processes involved in wine making.

The group listened attentively and with obvious interest as she talked. She told them as much as she could about the grapes that grew at Mountain View, how they were harvested in the fall and how they were crushed in a process that stripped the skins from the grapes and freed the juice in readiness for fermentation. The grapes were fermented according to the wines into which they would be made, with yeast added to start the process. The darker the final color of the wine, the longer the fermentation. Sulphite was added to the grapes to destroy the yeast cells and stop fermentation, as well as a twelve percent concentration of alcohol.

''Only twelve percent!'' a woman exclaimed, causing the others to laugh.

Only Albert remained poker-faced, Sara noticed, his eyes fixed on her face with unnerving concentration.

She would not let him intimidate her, she decided, as she went on talking. After fermentation, she explained, a substance called bentonite was added to the wine to clarify it. And after that, it was pumped into barrels for aging.

''Oak barrels, always,'' Sara told her fascinated audience. ''When I take you into the cellars, you'll see barrels that are two hundred years old and made of French oak.''

''How long does the wine age?'' one man asked.

''Depends on the wine. White wine can age from two months to a year. Red wines take at least four years or longer.''

It was time to go into the wineries. As they started to walk, Albert touched her arm. ''I never forget a face, Sara.''

The rest of the group heard every word he said.

''A great gift.'' Sara's coolness belied an inexplicable

nervousness. It made no sense that she wondered if Albert's persistence had something to do with Larry.

"I know you, Sara. Question is, where did we meet. How?"

"We've never met," Sara said flatly.

"This is my first trip west."

"There you are, then."

"Have you been east, Sara? Maine, perhaps?"

She stared at him mutely, her throat so dry that it was difficult to speak.

"Why don't you answer, Sara? Have you been east?" His tone was aggressive.

"I live in California," she said abruptly.

Someone more sensitive than Albert would have taken the hint. But the big, red-faced man continued his interrogation.

"You haven't said. Have you ever been to Maine? Lived there, maybe?"

She hesitated. "If I had, it wouldn't be your concern."

The momentary hesitation and the words she used were her undoing. "I knew it!" Albert exclaimed. "You were in Maine, and we did meet. How, Sara? When? Tell me."

"Albert," Mike intervened, "come and see something really interesting that—"

"Don't try and distract me." The florid man's tone was unpleasant. "Sara and I were just getting acquainted."

"We were not," she protested, a hint of fierceness audible beneath the surface.

"Keep it cool," Mike advised quietly, the remark intended for Sara's ears alone.

The rest of the group was starting to become interested. Many of them were staring at Sara, noticing her flushed cheeks and stormy eyes, their curiosity evident.

With some effort, she resumed the brightly impersonal voice of a guide. "At the end of the tour there'll be a wine tasting. You'll be able to sample the fine wines made on the estate. And for those who like to eat when they drink, there'll be crackers and cheese."

Her smile touched the faces of the group. "How does that sound?"

"Great!" someone exclaimed. "I've heard a lot about the wines of the Napa Valley, and I've been—"

"Got it!" Albert shouted.

Every face turned his way. As she saw the narrow eyes shining with undisguised malice, Sara suppressed a shiver of fear. She took a step backward.

"Got it!" he repeated. "I know why your face is familiar."

"You really have met, then?" one of the others asked.

"We haven't. Sara was right about that. It was a picture."

Sara stared at him blankly. "A picture?"

"In one of the newspapers down east."

"I've never appeared in any newspaper." It was a relief to know that Albert was mistaken.

"Some kind of scandal," he went on, undeterred.

The group stepped closer. "Scandal?" a man asked, his eyes gleaming.

"Right! Don't remember exactly what, but I'm pretty sure sex was involved."

"This is ridiculous!" Sara was outraged. "I've never been involved in any scandal."

"It was you," Albert insisted. "Don't remember the details, but some man was after you. You'd done something bad, and he was looking for you."

"You're quite mistaken." Sara's legs felt weak.

"What kind of scandal?" someone wanted to know.

"Is this true?" Mike asked in an undertone.

"Of course not!" Sara addressed the group. "I've never in my life been involved in a scandal, sexual or otherwise!"

But the people around her, Sara saw, were not convinced. The women were studying her warily. The men's eyes had turned speculative.

"I'm right!" Albert said, with obvious satisfaction. "I

know I am. Just wish I could remember the details. I will, though, give me time. My memory never fails me.''

With a sinking heart, Sara admitted he could be correct. While she knew of no picture, it would be just like Larry to do something that would humiliate her. The memory of his words was still raw in her mind. ''You'll go nowhere, Sara. If I can't have you, nobody will.'' Her parents had said he would do whatever he could to find her. And Larry had money and connections with the media.

What have you done, Larry? she wondered.

She had been right to get out of Maine, to find a place so remote from her old home that nobody would recognize her, a place where nobody would ever connect her with the man she had once imagined she loved and whom she now feared and hated.

What a cruel twist of fate that Albert should have seen her picture—if he had, in fact, seen it—and recognized her.

When she had shown the group through the upper area of the wineries—a collection of people who were no longer very interested in what she had to tell them about wine but were more interested in her own life and past—Sara led them down the flight of stone steps into the cellars.

The semidarkness was a welcome relief. Sara was unable to read her notes, but she had prepared herself so well that she didn't need them. With Albert and the others unable to see her flushed cheeks and distraught expression, she could concentrate on her talk.

She gasped when a hand brushed against her breast and looked quickly at the people closest to her. The men all met her gaze blandly. Blandest of all was Albert, his expression one of total innocence.

Sara bit back the accusation she had been about to make. They had been walking through the narrow aisles between the oak barrels. It would be the simplest thing in the world for someone to brush against her accidentally. No use getting paranoid.

On they went, with Sara still describing and explaining. She watched Albert deliberately while she talked. Let him know—in case he was up to any tricks—that she was on to him. But the gaze that met hers was as innocent as ever. A darn sight too innocent, Sara thought grimly.

And then it happened. Sara was between two barrels when someone kissed her. It was a quick kiss, lasting no more than a second.

Spinning around, she saw Albert hurrying away from her. She wasn't thinking as she went after him and slapped him hard across one cheek.

"How dare you!" Albert shouted.

"How dare *you?*" she countered furiously.

"Albert." Mike was at the man's side immediately. "Something happen?"

"This woman…this *slut* slapped me," Albert cried furiously.

"A misunderstanding, I'm certain," Mike said, comforting him. "Sara wouldn't have done a thing like that."

"I didn't make it up." The odious man sounded convincingly outraged.

"Why don't you ask him what *he* did to *me?*" Sara felt as if she would choke with anger.

"Didn't do a thing, don't know what the hell she's talking about." Albert seemed confused and puzzled.

"He kissed me," Sara told Mike.

Albert struck his forehead in pretended disbelief. "The woman is hallucinating! My God, Mike, what were you thinking of, bringing us here? The bitch flew at me like a tiger. And all because I remembered she'd been involved in a scandal."

"That isn't what happened." Tears pricked Sara's eyelids. But she couldn't let herself cry, not in front of all these people.

"Let's get on with the tour," Mike suggested.

His tone was so icy that Sara caught her breath. *I'm not at fault here,* she wanted to say. But she sensed that Mike wouldn't be interested.

As cheerfully as she could, she addressed the group. "We've reached the end of this part of the tour. We'll be going upstairs to the gift store. I hope you're all ready for crackers, cheese and wine? Some of you may even see things you'd like to purchase."

The group, many of them tired after a busy day of activities, perked up when they set eyes on the tempting array of food Sara had prepared before their arrival. She poured wine into small glasses, a small amount in each glass, so that people could taste more than one kind of wine, white wines and red and last of all champagne.

Albert, subdued and distant since Sara's outburst, ignored her and joined the others. Mike, Sara saw, had absented himself. He was attending to formalities with Sterling, she surmised.

The tour closed on a pleasant note. Mike appeared in the gift store, asked if his charges had had enough to eat and drink, and then they all followed him to the bus. With the exception of Albert, everyone said a friendly goodbye and thank-you to Sara.

Albert was the last to get on the bus. On the step he turned and looked at her directly. "There *was* a scandal." His expression was vindictive. "You haven't heard the end of this, Sara. I never forget a face. I didn't forget yours. And I won't forget what you did."

Sara didn't bother with an answer. She gave the man an impersonal look and was relieved when the bus left.

Her head was aching when she returned to the office. Emma kept a bottle of aspirin in her desk drawer, and Sara hoped she wouldn't mind if she helped herself to a couple.

She didn't notice Sterling until he turned from the window and said, "Well, Sara."

"Sterling! You startled me. I didn't realize you were here!"

"We need to talk."

His serious voice and expression told Sara that her or-

deal hadn't ended. She put a hand to a throbbing temple.
"Talk?"

He nodded.

"Does it have to be now, Sterling?"

"Yes, Sara, it does."

"Obviously, you know what happened."

"Some of it."

"Mike told you?"

"Of course."

"Well, then, you must know the details. There was this
obnoxious man. Albert. He molested me."

"What exactly did he do, Sara?"

"I thought," she said in a hard tone, "you already have
the story from Mike."

"I know what Mike told me. Now I want to hear it
from you."

"He kept harassing me verbally. In the cellars, I thought
he touched my breast, though I wasn't quite sure. Then
he kissed me."

Sterling's lips tightened, and in the firm jaw a muscle
moved. He looked so pale with anger that a relieved Sara
thought, *It's going to be okay.*

"He shouldn't have done that," Sterling said.

"No."

"And then you slapped his face." There was a different
note in his voice.

"That's right."

"Might have been better if you hadn't."

She stared at him disbelievingly. "A man molests me,
and *I'm* the one you blame?"

"I'm not blaming you, Sara. This guy, Albert, had no
right to touch you."

"But I shouldn't have slapped him? And here I thought
you'd understand." She bit out the words in disgust.

"Let me tell you what I understand." No change in the
even tenor of his voice. "Those people were guests at
Mountain View. Yes, Sara—" as she opened her mouth
to protest "—even Albert."

"This is ridiculous!"

"The man is a first-rate creep. And I agree, he deserved everything he got. But there can be a creep of one kind or another on any tour."

"You and Mike sound as if you got together and wrote the same guidebook," Sara said sarcastically. "I can't believe you'd expect me to allow men to paw me."

"I don't."

"I wouldn't, anyway. No matter what you said."

"You can't let men molest you, Sara. No man is allowed to do that."

"Then we're in agreement."

"Up to a point. As a tour guide, you need to find a way other than slapping to deal with obnoxious behavior. I can't tell you how. Your style has to be your own. Emma treats unwanted liberties with humor."

"*Humor!* Don't tell me she thinks it's funny when a man mauls her."

"Far from it. But over the years, Emma has acquired some very crushing put-downs. Her remarks are bitingly amusing—but only on the surface. What she says immediately puts the rest of the group on her side. And the man, the creep, ends up being the one who's humiliated."

"Can't say I think much of that method," Sara said stiffly.

"I've seen her do it, and I can tell you it's effective. No man would think of touching Emma twice." Sterling looked thoughtful. "There are other ways. You're going to have to find one that suits your particular personality."

Sara stared at him through stormy eyes. "I'm *appalled,* Sterling! I can't accept what I'm hearing—from the man who quit my job for me because someone pinched me."

"Don't think for a moment that I'm excusing what happened, Sara. I'm as furious as you are. Maybe more so. What I'm asking is that you find a different way of coping."

"You want me to go soft with pigs," she said contemptuously. "Albert is a pig, and so was Johnny in the diner."

"Wrong, Sara. That's not what I want."

"Maybe you should explain yourself."

"In the diner, when a man harassed you, you couldn't stand up for yourself. Your boss wouldn't let you. This is different. I *want* you to do something about it. I'd be angry if you didn't."

"I'm not sure I understand your point," Sara said slowly.

"Most tourists are respectful and courteous, but there are the few bad guys, and their behavior can cover the range from rudeness to touching. Neither Mike nor I ask you to keep silent, Sara."

"At this moment I don't know what you're asking. I don't believe we're even having this conversation."

He looked at her, brooding. "You don't seem to understand. I'm *glad* you stood up for yourself."

"That's not the impression you've been giving me since I walked in. I acted instinctively when I slapped the guy, Sterling. Besides, a woman doesn't always have a whole lot of options." Sara was thinking of Larry and wishing she had defended herself more forcefully against him.

"Granted. If some guy tries to force sex on you, I'd tell you to do whatever you can to defend yourself. Hit, kick, fight. Anything you can think of."

"Aren't you contradicting yourself?" she asked bitterly.

"I don't think so. When a tour member gets a bit too personal, when you have the security of other people around you, you can use a different method of rejection."

Sara's head ached more by the moment, but there were things that had not yet been said.

She looked at Sterling. "Mike was obviously displeased."

"Mike is in the tourist business, and he often has to put up with unpleasant people. But Mike is a professional, Sara, and he expects the same from us."

"What exactly are you saying?"

"He didn't condone Albert's behavior, you have to understand that. Far from it. At the same time, he made it clear that if anything like this happens again, he'll have to make arrangements with a different wine estate."

"A threat."

"More like a warning. Mike and I go back a long way together."

"You depend on the tours," Sara said slowly.

"They don't form the major part of my business. Wine is where I make most of my money. At the same time, tours are important to me."

And this job was important to Sara.

Dully, she said, "I don't want to ruin your business, so in future I'll find a better way of keeping my distance from the creeps."

"Glad to hear it." A small glimmer of amusement touched Sterling's eyes.

If only he would go now. She needed a painkiller. More than that, Sara needed to be alone. She had to think about the things Albert had said, about his threat and what it could mean.

But Sterling showed no signs of leaving. "Mike said something else, Sara."

Here it was—the real reason for their talk. She should have known, of course. The warnings about Albert had been the preliminaries. Who knew when there would be a tour, there would have been so much time for Sterling to talk to her about rejection.

"I can guess," she said tightly.

"Is it true, Sara?"

"No," she told him honestly. "There are things in every person's past, but I've never been involved in a scandal. Certainly not one of my making."

"Albert seemed to think he knew you from somewhere."

"Albert was wrong. And to my knowledge, I've never been mentioned in the media."

The fact that Larry might have found a way to publicize her leaving him was pure speculation.

"I see."

Sterling's eyes raked Sara's face, his gaze so intent, so questioning that she felt herself growing angry.

There was no stopping the two spots of color that stained her cheeks. "I already know the next question. You've wanted to know from the beginning whether I'm a woman on the run. I'm telling you—*again*—that I've done nothing criminal. No police officer will ever arrive here to arrest me."

There was the glimmer of a smile in Sterling's face. "You didn't need to tell me that, Sara. I know it. I've always known it. You couldn't do anything criminal if you tried."

She could tell from his voice that he meant it. The knowledge that he trusted her gave her a moment of intense pleasure.

"I just keep wondering if you're in trouble of some kind. If there's something I can do to help you."

"Nothing," she whispered.

He was at the door, but came to her. "Sara, according to Mike, he didn't think it could have been much of a kiss. As kisses go."

"That's true," she admitted.

"Even a small kiss upsets you?"

"You know it does. More than ever when it's from a man like Albert. He took a liberty, Sterling—no man is allowed to do that."

His hands came up to frame her face, his thumbs moving feather light over her cheeks. For some reason she was unable to pull away from him.

"I do know," he said softly. "If it's any consolation, I wish with all my heart it hadn't happened."

"How can I believe it? In light of all the other things you said, that whole long lecture about being polite to your guests."

"The lecture," Sterling said slowly, "was given in my

role as a businessman who understands the value of good customer relations. Even when they sicken me.''

"Obviously your business is more important to you than anything else.''

"No,'' Sterling told her quietly, "it may be an important part of my life, but there are other things that are even more important.''

"I don't know what you're saying.''

"Don't you, Sara?'' He smoothed a strand of hair from her forehead.

"No.'' Her voice shook.

"There's another part of me. I'm a man, Sara. A man who cares very much what happens to you.''

"So you say.'' It was hard to speak normally when the seductive hand was doing such alarming things to her senses.

"I do care, Sara. And because I do, I wish I'd been the one who hit Albert. I'd have hit him a lot harder than you did.''

For a moment she had a wild urge to throw herself into his arms. *Insane,* she told herself. *Thoroughly crazy.*

"I don't believe it,'' she said mockingly. "Such violent words from the man who depends on the goodwill of the tour companies.''

"Make of them what you will.''

He was so close to her that a clean, intensely masculine smell filled her nostrils. His hands were so big. His thumbs were beneath her chin, and his fingers reached all the way to her hairline. Sara shuddered with a treacherous longing that seemed to invade her whole body. Amazing that she could yearn for Sterling when she was repelled by Albert and Larry.

"Sterling...''

"I know, Sara, you're going to tell me you don't want me touching you.''

In fact, it wasn't at all what Sara had been about to say. When he dropped his hands and left the office, she didn't know whether she was disappointed or relieved that

Sterling's departure had prevented her from saying something she would have regretted.

She opened the desk drawer. Sometime she would have to think about Albert and his last-minute threat. But not now, not when what she needed more than anything else was a glass of water to wash down the aspirin.

CHAPTER SIX

SARA was in the garden when Sterling found her. Writing pad on lap, pen in hand, she was staring into the distance, obviously thinking. Since she hadn't noticed him, Sterling gave himself a few moments in which to enjoy looking at her.

She was as much a mystery to him as she had been the day he brought her to the Napa Valley. Maybe more so. The encounter with Albert in the wineries had unsettled her so greatly that for at least two days she had been as nervous as a newly broken horse. Sara had a secret, one she had no intention of discussing, and Sterling had decided he would not try to force it from her.

The only thing he knew for certain was that this very lovely woman had done nothing of which she could be ashamed. Just as certain was the fact that she intrigued him as no other woman had. Every day she seemed to grow more beautiful in his eyes. And every day he was drawn to her more intensely.

"Sara," he said at last.

She lifted her head quickly. "Why, Sterling..."

"Busy?"

She nodded. "Just writing something."

"A letter?" he asked lightly.

She hesitated. "To my parents."

"You never speak of them, Sara. Are they in California?"

"No." Her face assumed a shuttered look.

More mystery, Sterling thought, and decided not to continue with that particular line of questioning. When Sara was ready to talk, she would do so.

113

After a moment, she asked, "What can I do for you, Sterling?"

"You could go to a movie with me."

"A movie!" Gray eyes widened with surprise and also something that looked very much like relief.

"What did you think I wanted?" Sterling asked curiously.

"I keep thinking about that awful man, Albert. Wondering whether he'll lay an assault charge because I slapped him."

"He hasn't yet, and I don't expect he will."

"I'm not so sure, Sterling. Albert threatened me when he got on the bus, said I hadn't heard the end of it."

"I doubt he meant it, Sara. Albert sounds like the kind of guy who must have the last word at all times. Lots of bluster but no substance."

"You weren't there, Sterling. You didn't see his face, hear his voice. He isn't the kind to forgive and forget."

"Maybe not. But Albert knows he has things to answer for himself. If he decides to take action, we'll deal with it."

"We?" Sara asked, her eyes searching his. "You'd help me?"

"Sure," Sterling said easily. "We'd be in this together—didn't you know that?"

Gray eyes warmed, and the smile she gave him was tremulous. "I didn't— Thank you." She paused before saying, "And then there's Mike. I thought he might want me replaced."

She was so anxious, Sterling thought with a wave of compassion. This job was really important to her, and she didn't want to lose it.

"Don't worry about Mike. He made his point, and that's it. You'll be here until Emma gets back."

And after that, as well, he thought hopefully, but knew better than to say it.

"About the movie, Sara—will you go with me?"

"I don't know."

"Let me help you decide. Do you like action movies, Sara?"

Her eyes shone. "Adore them!"

"There's a new romantic thriller showing in town. I don't remember the title, but I can find out and get back to you."

"The title doesn't matter. It's ages since I last saw a movie. When were you thinking of going?"

"Tomorrow."

Sara hesitated, looking tempted yet torn. "You could go alone, Sterling."

"I prefer company."

"Isn't there someone else you could ask?"

"There is." He paused. "But I want to see it with you."

A mixture of unreadable expressions came and went in Sara's face. Just when Sterling was certain she would turn him down, she said, "I'll come, thank you."

"Tomorrow then. I'll leave you now so you can go on with your letter."

He was walking away when she said, "Sterling…"

"Too late to turn me down, Sara."

"It's not that. I… I just need to be sure you know where things stand."

"Where do they stand?" he asked very carefully.

"If I go with you, it isn't a date."

"What is it, Sara?"

"An outing. Employer and employee deciding to take in a movie together."

There it was again, the inexplicable fear of intimacy. If only he knew what caused it.

"Employer and employee sounds so formal, Sara."

"It's the way it has to be."

"Two friends sounds nicer."

"Friends," she agreed after a moment. "Nothing more than friendship, Sterling."

"Good friends?"

"Platonic."

"If you say so."

"I do."

"One day you might find yourself wanting more, Sara."

"I doubt it."

"Don't you ever experience sexual feelings?" he asked curiously.

"When will you understand that sex has no part in my life?" Her voice was so low that he thought he had frightened her.

"Never," he said cheerfully.

Sara moved restlessly in her chair. Her eyes were deep and troubled, and her lips quivered. She seemed to be in the grip of some intense emotion.

"Forget about the movie, Sterling."

He spoke gently so as not to frighten her further. "No way, Sara. We have an arrangement. You can't go backing down now."

"It isn't a good idea. Take that other person. Someone who'll be happy to go along with whatever you have in mind."

"I want to go with you," he said firmly.

"We'll go as two friends?"

"If that's what you want."

"Yes," she said, and he had the odd impression it wasn't the answer she really wanted to give.

"The movie starts at eight. We'll leave here at six-thirty."

He left the garden quickly, giving her no chance to change her mind.

There was quite a lineup by the time they arrived at the theater. People called out to Sterling, and Sara saw that he was well-known and well-liked in the town. He was especially well-liked by the women. More than one woman said a special kind of hello to him even at the risk of offending the man she was with. Sara noticed that looks were also directed her way, curious looks, as if people were interested in seeing Sterling's date.

Not his date, just a friend, she reminded herself firmly.

They found two seats near the back. As Sara sat down, she was careful to be as far as she could from Sterling. She had a light sweater with her, and she put it over her lap and her hands in a way that she hoped seemed casual. Unless Sterling was brazen, he would make no move to take her hand.

Moments after she dropped the sweater, he turned his head and winked. Okay, Sara thought grimly, so he knew what she was up to. So what? They had agreed on Platonic companionship.

She was glad when the movie began. Almost from the start she was gripped by the story. Part fast-paced action movie, part romance, it seemed to have all the elements that made for entertaining theater.

The heroine was lovely and spirited. It was easy to see why the hero was attracted to her. As for the hero, he would be the stuff of many a woman's dreams. Good-looking, tough and sexy. A man any woman would fall in love with. Very much like Sterling. Without thinking, Sara glanced at the man beside her.

As if he felt her gaze, he turned to her. The breath caught in her throat as a current seemed to go from his body to hers. In that moment, she longed to put her hand in his. It took an effort of will to keep it safely beneath her sweater.

On the screen, the drama intensified. So thrilling was the action that Sara stopped thinking of Sterling and was caught up in the movie.

The hero and the heroine were in the throes of a tender love scene while outside, unseen, the bad guys drew closer. A tender parting, a promise to meet again soon, and then the hero was pulling on his clothes and leaving. On the street, a sinister man gave a signal.

Sara sat forward in her seat. The excitement was building by the moment, the tension on the screen communicating itself to the audience. To a person, the theater was filled with people who were waiting for a climax.

The bad guys closed in suddenly. The hero was pinned against a wall. Sara's heart leaped in her throat. The tension was unbearable. *Let him get out of this alive.* Sara wasn't thinking as she flung a hand from under her sweater and gripped one of Sterling's hands tightly.

A second passed, and then his hands folded around hers. It was only minutes later, when the tension had eased somewhat—the hero had managed to get away from his assailants—that Sara became aware of what she had done.

On the screen, the movie played on. There was a part of Sara that was still watching the action. But there was another part, too, a stronger part, that was solely conscious of the hand holding hers. A big hand, warm and vital, its fingers threading through hers, communicating a message more effectively than words. It was a message that set off a tingling in every nerve of Sara's body. A message that made her pulsate with longing. Passionate woman that she had once been—and was still—she recognized the throb of physical attraction, the yearning for intimacy, the pure sexual hunger.

She longed to lean into Sterling's body, to unbutton his shirt and rub her cheek against his chest. At the same time, she understood how important it was not to do it.

She had to withdraw from him, had to break the spark created by their linked hands. She tried. That was what she would tell herself later. She really did try to move her hand. But nothing happened.

''No!'' she whispered.

''You started this,'' he whispered back.

He wasn't telling her anything she didn't know. Still, she depended on him to help her. ''Let go, Sterling.''

Angry murmurs started around them. Sterling put his mouth to Sara's ear. ''Enjoy it,'' he whispered, his voice entering her directly, privately, so quietly that nobody but Sara would hear him.

She was already very excited. His lips were on her ear-lobe, and just for a second, his tongue caressed her ear.

Sara thought she would pass out with longing and arousal. She was not even thinking about their linked hands. There was only the craving to be on Sterling's lap, to wind her arms around his neck, to feel his kisses on her mouth and throat.

She had to control herself. Had to force her attention to the screen. Once more, she tried, and failed, to withdraw her hand. But she did manage to move her head sideways, out of Sterling's reach, and even that was a mammoth achievement.

Somehow, by sheer strength of will, and with that big, warm hand still holding hers, she managed to watch the rest of the movie. In the best tradition of happy endings, the hero survived all obstacles and returned to the heroine, bloodied and bruised but with his pride intact and his love for his woman as strong as ever.

If the ending was predictable, it was also heartwarming and believable. Sara, whose one major relationship had been so unhappy, vicariously experienced the final joy and sadness of the two screen lovers. When they were finally able to declare their love for each other, she was weeping.

"Are you okay?" Sterling whispered.

She could only nod. He dabbed at her eyes with a tissue, and she didn't have the strength to stop him. When he put his arm around her shoulder and held her close, she did not resist him. Just this once, she didn't want to be strong. She needed the comfort of Sterling's closeness.

When the movie ended and Sterling suggested going to a restaurant for coffee and dessert, Sara was still too weak from emotion to protest. Besides, she was enjoying this evening more than she had dreamed she would. Might as well end it on a high note.

They found a place a few blocks from the theater. It was full, but it seemed Sterling was known there, and a table was found in a secluded alcove. Together they pored

over the dessert menu and found that neither of them cared
for crème caramel.

"Mushy stuff," Sterling observed, wrinkling his nose
as he said it.

Sara laughed. "Slides over your plate when you dig
your spoon in it."

"I know people who like it."

"I know people who'd die for it."

"Give me carrot cake any day," Sterling said as he read
the menu.

"I *love* carrot cake!"

"How about chocolate cake?"

"Mmm, I like that, too!"

"Shall we order one of each and share?"

"Great idea!"

"Coffee or cappuccino?"

"Oh…cappuccino for a treat."

When Sterling had ordered, he said, "We have things
in common, you and I, Sara."

"Because we both hate crème caramel and like the
same cake and cappuccino?"

"It's a sign, don't you think?"

Again, Sara laughed, and Sterling laughed, too. It was
surprisingly easy, and so very nice, to be able to laugh
with him. Sara couldn't remember the last time she and
Larry had shared a laugh. In those last weeks, particularly,
there had been nothing to laugh about.

"A sign?" she asked. "*That's* what you call a sign?"

"Sure," Sterling said with mock seriousness. "Signs
can be anything, anywhere. How many people do you
know who like the same cake?"

"There must be thousands, Sterling! Millions."

"But when you throw in crème caramel and cappuccino?"

She decided to play along with him. "That does alter
the picture." And again she was laughing.

They talked about the movie, the plot and the characters. There was so much to talk about. When they dis-

agreed on some point, the discussion was spirited but friendly. And that, too, was different from Sara's experiences with Larry. Larry was always right, no matter what. That being the case, there was nothing much to debate or discuss.

When they had apportioned the cake, half slices of chocolate and carrot cake on each plate, Sterling leaned across the table.

"Sara... Why did you cry?"

"The movie was sad."

"Not that sad."

"Emotional, then."

"So emotional that it would make you cry so hard?"

The laughter left Sara's face as she felt herself going on the defensive. "I bet other women were crying, too."

"I think they were. But not quite as hard as you."

Sara's muscles grew rigid. Once before, Sterling had lulled her into going somewhere with him. They had had a lovely picnic by the side of a bubbling creek, but the moment she'd relaxed her guard, the interrogation had started. Had she allowed the same thing to happen again?

Before she could stop him, Sterling reached for her hand.

"Don't!"

"You didn't mind in the theater."

"That was different. Please, let go of my hand, Sterling."

He brought it to his lips and kissed it instead. A shiver ran up Sara's arm, but she tried to ignore it.

"Tell me why you cried."

"I've already told you—it was emotional. Perhaps I did cry more than others, but things affect people differently."

But that wasn't the answer, and Sara knew it. She had wept for the characters in the movie, but more than that, she had wept for herself, for all the things she had kept suppressed for so long. It had taken the movie to uncork the bottle of her emotions.

She had wept for a baby conceived without love, a baby

that would never know the father who'd rejected it. She had wept for the abuse she had suffered at Larry's fists, for the blackmail to which she had surrendered and for her beloved parents, who must be so confused by her unexplained disappearance.

And she had wept for Sterling and for a love that would never be hers to enjoy. Sara was in love with Sterling, she knew that. It had happened despite her resolve to remain aloof from him. And it could have no happy ending. Emma would be back soon, the job would end, Sara would have to move on—and Sterling would be out of her life forever.

"That's all there is to it?" Sterling asked.

"That's all," she agreed, though her throat ached with more tears.

On the way to Mountain View, Sterling seemed to sense Sara's need for silence. She stared into the darkness, pushing down hard on tears that threatened to fall.

"I'll walk you to the house," he said when he'd parked the car.

"No need," she countered, a little brusquely.

"I make a habit of accompanying a woman to her door after a date."

A date. There it was again, the reference to his socializing. If only it didn't hurt so much to know that there were other women in Sterling's life.

"It wasn't a date," she reminded him, her voice low.

"Wasn't it?" he asked lazily.

"You know what we said beforehand."

"What *you* said, Sara. It seemed very much like a date when we were holding hands."

Sara didn't answer because she couldn't.

At the door of her little house, she said, "Thanks for a lovely evening."

"It isn't over." With those words, Sterling took her hand and drew her into the house with him.

Seconds later, he was kissing her. A light kiss, not much

more than a brushing of her lips, yet so erotically tantalizing that the blood turned to fire in Sara's already burning veins.

After a minute or so, he lifted his head and looked at her. ''That wasn't so bad, was it?''

She thought her love must be in her eyes as she looked at him—but she knew how important it was for her to deny it.

''Why?'' It was all she could manage to say.

''Why did I kiss you?''

She nodded.

''I wanted to,'' he said.

''Even though you know how I feel about it?''

Sterling held her a little away from him so he could look at her properly. His gaze was searching, penetrating. It seemed to reach, Sara thought despairingly, all the way to her heart.

''I know what you tell me,'' he said at last, ''but I don't believe it.''

''You must.''

''How can I, Sara? You tell me one thing, but your body and your responses keep saying something different.''

''No!''

''You know it's so, sweetheart. Every time.''

Sweetheart?

''You're wrong, Sterling. I've told you from the start how I feel about intimacy. It was one of the conditions of my coming here.''

''Things change, Sara.''

''Not always,'' she said faintly.

She tried to push herself out of his arms, but he was holding her with surprising firmness. Even then, she should have been able to get free from him—she wasn't some weakling, after all—but as had happened previously, her brain seemed incapable of sending the right signals to her limbs.

Softly, Sterling said, "Can you tell me, honestly, that you hated the kiss?"

How could she say it and sound convincing? How could she say it when she had savored every second?

If only she could let herself surrender to the pleasure of the moment. But she knew so little about Sterling's true character, and she'd had enough trauma to last her a lifetime.

There was nothing for it but to retreat to the safety of her first question. "Why did you kiss me, Sterling?"

"Because the time is right." He put a finger against her lips as she opened her mouth to speak. "I know you're frightened."

"I...I'll always feel this way, Sterling."

"No, Sara, you won't. I'll teach you not to."

God, the words were exciting, stirring up incredible images in her mind. Sex with Sterling would be fantastic. She was in love with him. She could imagine herself *making* love with him. Sara closed her eyes.

She had thought herself in love with Larry, too. That was the thought that caused her eyes to snap open again. Sara had been so certain that Larry was the man she would love all her life. Instead, Larry had taught her there was not a man in the world she could trust.

The thought gave her the strength to push herself away from Sterling.

"I think you should go," she said.

"Not yet."

"Sterling, please."

His face changed, the expression in his eyes deepening. "If you could have heard your voice when you said that. If you were any other woman, I'd think you were asking me to make love to you."

He was so close to the truth. She did want to make love with him. But she knew she couldn't.

"You know better than that," Sara said faintly.

"What I know," Sterling said after a long moment,

"is that you're very innocent. Vulnerable. I don't know whether you're untouched because—"

"Sterling, stop!"

"There may be a reason for your fear. Something you're not telling me."

Sara took another step back. "This is crazy!"

"Is it, Sara?"

"Yes. And it really is time for you to go."

But the man she loved showed no signs of moving. The eyes looking at her were dark and enigmatic, and when he spoke his voice was husky.

"I won't go before I've said what's on my mind. You want to know why I kissed you, Sara? Okay. One reason is because I want to show you that kissing can be fun. That lovemaking between a man and a woman can be the most wonderful thing in the world. I want to prove to you that there's nothing to be scared of."

The words made Sara's head swim. "You said, one reason." She held her breath as she waited for Sterling to continue.

"The other—I want to get to know you better. You must know I'm attracted to you, Sara." His voice was low and a little rough.

"I wish you wouldn't talk this way!" The words tumbled out in a mixture of panic and excitement.

"Don't worry, Sara, I won't rush you into anything. We'll take things slowly."

As he drew her into his arms, Sara was swept by a great rush of love. But she was frightened, too, so terribly frightened. She trembled as he drew her against him, a trembling that grew stronger as she felt the hard length of his body.

"I'm not going to hurt you," Sterling whispered, and Sara knew he had felt her trembling.

Once more, he cupped her face. As he searched her eyes, one hand left her face and went to her hair, his fingers threading through it. The sensations he was stirring in her made Sara tremble more than ever. She closed her eyes so Sterling would not see the depths of her desire, and a rough sound escaped his throat.

Then he was pulling her against him. As he began to kiss her again, Sara sensed the passion this giant of a man was trying so hard to contain. His kisses were sweet and tender, but after a few minutes they became firmer, harder, more passionate, an onslaught that made her weak with a longing for more. It was as though he could only contain himself so far and no further.

Inside Sara a battle was waging. There was the ever-present fear of being hurt by a man, and then there was her wild passion and a hunger that was so deep she didn't know how much longer she could fight it.

Sterling groaned as Sara opened her lips and allowed his tongue to explore her. For long moments there was only sensation. Sara felt as if she was rapidly losing her mind as Sterling made love to her mouth and as his body throbbed against hers. So deep was her hunger she wasn't thinking as she lifted her hands to his neck, pushing her fingers below his collar to the strong muscles of his shoulders, then up to his hair, reveling in the feel of the springiness beneath her fingers.

Sterling was the one to call a sudden halt. As he lifted his head, Sara could only stare at him, her eyes dazed and shocked.

"Sara... Oh, God, Sara, have you any idea how exciting you are?"

Numbly, she shook her head.

"You're all woman, sweetheart. Beautiful and desirable. A woman made for a man to love."

From some recess of Sara's brain a memory returned. *A woman made for a man to love.* The words Larry had said in the early days of their relationship, when he was trying to seduce her into believing that he really loved her. And now Sterling was saying the same words. It was not to be endured!

"You don't know what you're talking about!" she cried. "This shouldn't have happened."

"Sara! Sara, what's wrong?"

"How can you ask me that? You know how I feel, and you tried to force me to make love."

Sterling looked stunned. Then his lips tightened, and a hard look came into his face. "I didn't force you to do anything."

"We were just going to see a movie. No date, that's what we said. Where did you mean this to end?"

"I was the one who stopped," he reminded her harshly.

"Temporarily." Her breath was coming in gasps.

"What the hell are you trying to say, Sara?"

"You just stopped for a moment. But we'd have gone on again sooner or later."

"Not necessarily."

"I know we would! No man ever stops before he has what he wants."

"I thought you were inexperienced." Sterling's expression was so odd as he searched her face. "You're a virgin, Sara, how do you know what men want?"

Sara's hands clenched at her sides. Careful, she told herself, as she tried to take a calming breath. She was so close to saying the wrong thing.

"There are things a woman knows," she said at last.

"Such as what? That all men are brutes? That we only live to satisfy our crass urges?"

She couldn't meet his eyes. "Something like that."

Now it would come, the tongue-lashing, the furious response. Perhaps, like Larry, Sterling would hit her. If he did, she would hit back. The days when she would suffer a man's abuse were over. She might not be as strong as Sterling, but if he tried to hurt her, she would fight like a wildcat. She was in love with Sterling—but she had thought herself in love with Larry, too. She would never let Sterling or any other man hurt her.

But Sterling didn't try to hurt her. In fact, when he spoke again, his tone was surprisingly quiet. "You're even more frightened than I realized."

"Maybe I am."

"We're not all animals, Sara."

"Are you saying you don't want sex, Sterling?" She threw the words at him furiously.

"I'm not saying that at all."

"At least you're honest!"

His eyes met hers steadily. "I would like to make love to you—I'm not denying it. I want it very much. But when we make love it will be because we both want it."

"It won't happen!" If only the shaking of her voice didn't give the lie to her words.

"Don't be so sure, sweetheart. You keep surprising me, Sara. You're far more passionate than you like to let on."

"Sterling…"

"I know you don't want to believe it. It's because you're frightened, but I'm determined to help you get over your fear. You will want to make love, Sara, and I'm willing to wait for that day."

Two hours later, Sara was still awake. Tossing and turning had reduced her bed to chaos. The sheets were crumpled, the blanket half on the bed, half on the floor.

There would be no sleep for her tonight, she realized, as she went to the window and stared into the fog hanging over the hills and the dark vineyards. Her mind was in turmoil, her body racked with longing.

The cause of her restlessness was simple enough. The solution, if there was one, was more difficult.

The decision to leave Larry had been agonizing. There was a baby to think of, Larry's baby, even if he was a furious and unwilling father. There was her father to consider. Had it not been for Larry's threats to have her dad fired after thirty years with the company, Sara would have left Larry the first time he hit her.

But she had made the decision, and though the consequences had been difficult, she had been certain if she could only find a job and save some money, she would be able to cope with her baby and her life.

The last thing she had expected was that she would fall

in love. Deeply, passionately in love. So much in love that her body hungered with the need to be with Sterling. He would never know how difficult it had been for her to see him leave her house when all she really wanted was to let him take her to bed.

Yet all the while, on the periphery of her fast-fading sanity, had been the knowledge that she could not let it happen. Sterling talked of her fear of sex. What he did not know was that what she really feared was men.

On the surface, Sterling was exceptional. Apart from his dynamic looks and vibrant sex appeal, he had qualities any woman would admire, strength, confidence and toughness. And those other qualities, integrity, tenderness and compassion.

It was so tempting to put her trust in Sterling. Yet again and again, one thought returned. She had seen him only in good situations. How would he behave if he was displeased or upset?

How could she know that Sterling would be any different from Larry?

CHAPTER SEVEN

THE library was a cheerful, whitewashed building with creepers growing over the walls to the roof. The interior was attractive, with colorful posters and plants and comfortable reading areas placed discreetly between the shelves of books.

Sara headed straight for the newspaper area with its selection of out-of-state publications, many of them a little dog-eared, testimony to the multitude of tourists who yearned for news of home when they were traveling.

Last time she had visited the library, the paper she'd wanted had been unavailable. But there it was today, a Maine daily wedged between the *New York Times* and a Missouri weekly. In a quiet reading area, Sara spread the paper in front of her.

Ever since the afternoon in the wineries when the obnoxious Albert had been so certain he'd seen her face somewhere, Sara had known what she must do. This particular newspaper might not be the right one, but it was a popular Maine publication, and as such it was a good place to start.

She skimmed the first pages, barely taking in the news of the murder trial that had been on people's lips for months or the latest political scandal. All she did was scan the headlines and glance at the advertisements.

She was almost at the end and was beginning to think she could relax when she let out a gasp. For a heart-stopping moment she stared at a picture of herself surrounded by the thin black lines of an advertisement. She recognized the photo immediately. It had been taken by Larry in a time when Sara had believed herself to be happy, loved and in love.

130

Above her face was a caption. Have You Seen This Woman? And then the real shocker, a thousand-dollar reward to the person who revealed Sara's whereabouts.

One thousand dollars! Larry must have taken leave of his senses. Only a driven man bent on getting his way no matter what could have stooped so low. *Have you seen this woman?* The words made her sound like a criminal.

Sara's thoughts went to Albert. The awful man had talked of an article, not an advertisement. Remembering Larry's media connections, Sara understood that he must have started with a press release of some kind. Had the article mentioned a reward? Probably not, because if it had, Albert would have had no hesitation in informing the tour group that Sara was a woman with a price on her head. The reward must have been a refinement Larry had come up with later.

It didn't take much imagination to picture the article Larry would have written. Woman Missing. Prominent Executive Frantic, the headline would have read. The details would have been lurid, painting Sara in a shocking light, while at the same time extolling Larry, the devoted, deceived and tormented lover, desperate to learn the whereabouts of the shameless woman who had left him.

No wonder Albert had connected Sara with a scandal. Feeling ill, unable to look at the ad a moment longer, Sara closed the paper.

For a while she sat quite still. Had the time come to leave the Napa Valley, to get away before Albert or anyone else could go to Larry with information about her?

She felt sick at the very thought of leaving Mountain View before her time there was up. She was so happy at the wine estate. She hated to be deprived of even one day there.

More than anything, she could not bear to part from Sterling. To walk away from him now would be like ending her life before she had to. Emma was due back in six weeks. Who knew what would happen after that? It wasn't impossible that Sterling might recommend Sara to someone else in the valley who needed a secretary.

Besides, she had given Sterling her commitment. There was no way she could walk out on him now. He would be understandably furious if she left him in the lurch, and she couldn't bear the thought of his contempt.

In any event, it made no sense to go elsewhere. Wherever she went, there would be more newspapers, more advertisements, other people who might recognize her. Larry was a wealthy man. He did not have to limit himself to the media of one state. He could advertise nationwide. Sara could not run forever—she knew that.

"Finished with that?" A passing librarian was looking at the folded paper.

"Yes, I am," Sara said, her voice just louder than a whisper. The librarian looked at her curiously, and Sara thought, *She knows who I am.*

"From the east coast originally, are you?"

After a moment, she said, "That's right."

"Figured you must be, since this publication is from Maine. Next one's due in tomorrow. Come and look at it if you're interested."

Something in the way the woman said it made Sara realize the librarian was just being friendly. *I'm becoming paranoid.*

"I might do that," she said, calmer, yet knowing very well that since she didn't want her face to become familiar, it was unlikely she would ever be back.

"I was wondering..." She stopped.

"Yes?"

"All these out-of-state papers. I know they're for the tourists, but do the people from around here read them, too?"

"Lord, no. Takes long enough just to read the local stuff and the major national and international news. Not to mention sports and fashion and the comics. Some of the really big ones are always popular, of course—papers like the *New York Times* or the *Washington Post*. But if you're talking simple out-of-state publications, I don't think any of the Napa Valley crowd would be interested.''

Thank goodness for that! Albert had been the worst of bad luck, but if the librarian was correct, it was unlikely anyone else would see her picture and go to Larry with information and a request for the reward. With any luck, Sara could relax, secure in the knowledge that she was safe.

But she had to talk to Sterling. True, she didn't owe him any explanations, and if she dressed carefully, she would be gone from Mountain View before the pregnancy became visible. Nevertheless, there was a part of her that knew she had kept the story of her past from him long enough. Too long, perhaps.

Knowing what she had to do didn't make the thought of talking any easier. She was desperately in love with Sterling Tayler, and she longed to have that love returned. What she dreaded was pity. Yet pity was probably what she would get from him. Pity, and maybe contempt.

Sara rose early the next morning, showered and dressed quickly, then left her house before she could change her mind. With any luck, Sterling would not have departed for the vineyards yet.

As always, at this time of morning, the air was sweet and fresh, with the shrubs surrounding the house sending out a strong scent. It didn't rain in summer in California, and the heat turned the grass from winter green to brown, but Sterling had chosen the shrubs carefully, picking only those that flourished without much water.

Normally, Sara loved the early morning, but not today. As she walked toward the main house, she could only think of Sterling and wonder how he would react to her story.

There was no response when she rang the bell. She waited a few seconds, then rang again. Still nothing. Sterling must have left the house earlier than usual, she thought, and began to walk away.

"Sara."

She turned. "I thought you had already—" The words stopped in her throat as he opened the door wide.

Sterling stood in the doorway, a towel around his waist. His hair was tousled, and his arms and chest glistened wetly.

He had never looked sexier. In an instant, a hot flood of desire invaded Sara's loins. She longed to go to him, to fold her arms around his neck, to press herself against him and beg him to make love to her. She had never wanted him quite as much as she did at this moment.

"Sara." His eyes gleamed as if he knew exactly the effect he was creating. "This is a surprise."

"Surprise?" She could hardly speak.

"Have you come for breakfast?"

"Of course not."

Somehow, she managed to take a couple of steps backward, as if by distancing herself from him she could lessen the impact he was having on her. Not that it worked. She wanted him just as much. But at least from a distance, Sterling would not see the glazed look she suspected was in her eyes, might not hear her breathing, which was a little too fast.

"Did I get you out of the shower?" Her voice was choked.

"You could say that. I was turning off the water when I heard the bell. Did you ring more than once?"

"Twice, actually."

"If you didn't come for breakfast, why are you here? To shower with me?"

"*Sterling!*"

"Sorry," he said cheerfully, without looking in the least apologetic. "I keep forgetting how modest you are." His eyes gleamed with devilment. "But we could shower together anyway. I'm still wet, and I don't mind going back in."

The mere thought of standing under streaming hot water

with Sterling sent shock waves of excitement scudding through her system.

"That's absurd!" she protested jerkily.

"It isn't, really." He took a step toward her and touched her cheek with a damp finger. "You can't begin to imagine how fantastic it can be for a man and woman to shower together, soaping each other, kissing—"

"Sterling, don't!"

The problem was that she could imagine it all too well, and the idea was so tempting that if she didn't gain control of her emotions very quickly, she might just end up accepting the invitation.

"Sara...Sara, sweetheart, you can't be a virgin forever."

Sweetheart. If only the endearment meant something, but Sara knew it was probably loosely said. Briefly she closed her eyes, then opened them.

The damp finger moved to her mouth, tracing an erotic path around her lips. "You don't know what you're denying yourself," Sterling said softly. "You can't avoid men all your life, Sara. Don't you know that?"

But she knew it was what she had to do—avoid men, shield herself from danger, from any possible hurt. If only she hadn't fallen in love. It made no sense at all that she wanted this one man so much.

"Let's not get into this again," she said roughly.

Sterling subjected her to a long and very searching study, one that encompassed her face and her throat before descending to the rest of her body. It took all Sara's willpower to remain still.

When his eyes lifted to her face once more, she tried for sarcasm. "Are you quite finished?"

"No. But this will have to do for the moment."

"Then I'll be on my way."

"You came here for a reason. What was it, Sara?"

She remembered the thing that had gone temporarily out of her mind. "I need to talk to you."

His eyes glinted. "Sounds serious."

"It is."

"What is it, Sara?"

The superb male figure drew her eyes like a magnet. No other man could be as virile and as sexy as Sterling.

"I can't talk like this," she muttered.

"You said it was serious."

"We—we can talk later in the office."

"I have a better idea," Sterling said. "Have dinner with me tonight."

"Dinner?"

"We can talk then."

"I don't think so, Sterling."

"My housekeeper is off today, so she won't be here to cook. Do you like barbecues?"

"Love them!" The words were out before she could stop them.

"Great. Sevenish, Sara?" Once more he touched her face. "You're having second thoughts, I can see the doubt in your eyes. But since I won't take no for an answer, it's a date. See you at seven."

It required a strength Sara didn't have to refuse him. She could only nod.

As Sara rinsed the shampoo out of her hair, she really did feel as if she was getting ready for a date. *A date.* Some of the feelings she'd experienced as a teenager, about to go out with a boy the first time, came rushing back to her—the nervousness, the dry mouth, the tingling excitement. The slight sense of insecurity. *Will he like what I'm wearing? Will he like me? What will we talk about? Will he try and kiss me? What do I do if he does?*

Contradictory thoughts, given the fact that she and Sterling were going to have a very serious and unpleasant talk. Given too, that he might never look at her in the same way afterward.

Still, as she stepped out of the shower, Sara felt as tremulous, as filled with sexual anticipation as a young woman who had never before been alone with a young man.

She toweled her hair until it was almost dry, then brushed it lightly in a way that was quite different from the crisp no-nonsense back-from-the-face style she'd adopted since coming to work for Sterling.

Before she dressed, she looked at herself in the mirror. Although it would still be a while before she had to wear bigger clothes, her body had changed since her arrival at the wine estate. Her breasts were filling out, and her belly had a very small curve, so slight as to be unnoticeable to anyone except herself, but a curve nonetheless.

Soon she would start to feel the baby moving inside her. Her darling baby, which she loved already, despite its dreadful father and despite the obstacles that lay ahead.

There were decisions she would have to make. Important decisions. But there was still time to make them. So much depended on where she went when this job ended. There was no point in trying to decide on a doctor and a hospital, on the many other necessary details, until she knew where she would be living when she left Mountain View.

With a sensuousness that was foreign to her, she slipped on a soft crimson shirt and a cream skirt she hadn't worn for months, even though it was one of her favorites. A narrow belt cradled a still tiny waist, though it was buckled one notch looser than the last time she'd worn it.

Sara had taken little jewelry with her when she'd fled Larry's home, but she did have the topaz pendant that had been her grandmother's, and there were small gold studs in her ears.

Sterling opened the door at the first knock, the welcoming smile freezing on his face as he looked at her.

"Something wrong?" Sara whispered.

"Wrong! Heavens, no! How can you even think such a thing?" His voice was gruffer than she had ever heard it.

"I just wondered." His very male look brought a note of teasing into Sara's tone.

"You look—stupendous, Sara! Like a model. A movie

star. I'd like to skip dinner and just carry you to bed and make love to you.''

''Sterling!''

''Don't say it, sweetheart. I know it's not what you want. Let's just think about the barbecue. I'm hoping you'll do the food justice for a change.''

First, though, he said, as he led her on to the patio, they would have a cocktail.

''You know I don't drink.''

''Tonight will be the exception,'' he told her with a smile. ''You'll like it, I promise.''

''Thanks—but no. I mean that.''

''You won't mind if I have one?''

''Of course not,'' she said with a smile. ''But I will have some of that juice I see in that jug over there.''

Sara sat in her chair as Sterling filled two glasses and handed her one. The sky was very beautiful with the colors of sunset. Over the hills one lonely air balloon still drifted, and on a high cliff a big bird hovered, a hawk, Sterling said.

A hawk, a bird of prey. Sara thought of Larry and swallowed hard.

Tearing her eyes from the bird and the sunset, she looked at Sterling. ''I told you I needed to talk.''

''About the office?'' he asked cheerfully. ''You've got the files all mixed up. How dreadful.''

''They're in perfect order, and it's not that.''

''You wiped some vital information off the computer, and there's no backup. Even worse.''

His eyes sparkled with such mischief that Sara was sorely tempted to play along with his nonsense. But she was here for a purpose.

''It's not the office, Sterling.''

''You robbed a bank when you were in town yesterday, and now you want me to help you spend the money.''

''I wish you'd be serious, Sterling.''

''Perhaps,'' he said, ''I don't want to be serious.''

"But there's something I've been meaning to tell you, and I—"

"We've covered all the serious issues—there can't possibly be anything else."

"Sterling."

"Not tonight, Sara. We were just starting to have a good time. Whatever it is, it can wait till tomorrow."

"Tomorrow you'll think up some other excuse not to hear me."

"Tomorrow we'll talk, I promise."

"In other words, you lured me here under false pretenses."

"Lured. Now there's an interesting word." Again, his eyes sparkled. "What else can I lure you into, Sara?"

"Not a thing. Don't even think about it. About our talk, Sterling—"

"Tomorrow," he repeated. "Let's just enjoy tonight, Sara."

Sterling was in no mood to be serious. Feeling as if she'd been granted a wonderful reprieve, Sara decided she would allow herself to enjoy the evening as he suggested. Time enough tomorrow for the talk that could no longer be postponed.

At the edge of the patio, a wisp of smoke rose from the barbecue. Sterling had made the fire some time ago—not for him, it seemed, the gas barbecues that most people seemed to use these days—and the flames were low enough for him to put on the meat.

"You're a man of many talents," Sara said when he handed her a plate with steak, a crisply warmed bun and a green salad.

"Thanks." He lifted his glass. "Time for a toast. What will it be, Sara?"

She knew what she would drink to if she could—love, a life with Sterling, a home for her baby on this lovely estate. All of it a dream, one that would never be hers.

"I'm not good at toasts, Sterling. Do you have one?"

"I do, indeed. I'd like to drink to the most beautiful woman in the world."

The eyes that held hers were unusually deep and dark. Sara's heart began a crazy thumping.

"Do I know her, Sterling?"

"She's sitting across the table from me."

If only she were free to enjoy this lighthearted talk!

As lightly as she could, she said, "I think you're flirting with me, Sterling—for a change."

"It's not all I want to do with you, Sara."

I want it, too. More than you can imagine!

"Do you often entertain women?" she asked.

"You're changing the subject."

"Am I?"

"You know you are. Do you feel safer when you can pretend that lovemaking isn't a part of your life?"

"What makes you think I'm pretending?" She did not meet his eyes.

"Aren't you, sweetheart?"

That endearment again. "I think you know the answer to that." She paused. "The meal is great, Sterling. The steak's soft as butter."

"Is that why you're smiling?"

"Am I?" She could feel the upward tilt of her lips. "I guess it's because I'm enjoying myself."

"Then I've achieved what I set out to do."

"What do you mean, Sterling?"

"You've looked unusually tense since you got back from town yesterday. And earlier, when you wanted to talk."

"Did I?"

"You know you did. Why, Sara?"

She shot him a mischievous look. "Does it matter?"

"You tell me, Sara."

"Lord, Sterling, you were the one who wasn't in the mood for serious talk."

"Maybe this really is the time for it. What if I said I'd changed my mind?"

Sara grinned at him. "Maybe now I've changed mine."

"Then you don't want to talk?"

"Not tonight."

She was telling him no more than the truth. It was as if, after the delicious meal and the lovely toast, all her tension had vanished. The things that had seemed so earth-shakingly important—the ominous advertisement, the abuse and the blackmail—were not quite so important now. They were topics that could easily wait until tomorrow.

"I'm glad you feel that way," Sterling said. "It means we can enjoy the evening after all."

When they had both had their fill, he came to her side of the table. "Come, Sara."

She stood up without argument. "Where to?"

"Let's walk."

"In the dark?"

"In the moonlight. Look over there, Sara." He gestured. "A full moon tonight."

"I'd noticed. Shouldn't we do the dishes first?"

"They'll wait."

She let him take her hand as they left the patio and walked into the garden.

For a while they walked in silence, a silence that seemed to accentuate their closeness. Sara was acutely aware of the large hand holding hers, of the muscular body brushing against her in the darkness.

"Sara—are you going to let me kiss you?"

The words sent an immediate throbbing through the lower part of Sara's body. She loved this man—passionately, deeply, crazily—and she longed for his kisses. If truth be told, she wanted far more than that.

He had been holding her hand quite loosely, but as they walked, their fingers interwove. Later, Sara could not have said who started the process. All she knew was that it was sheer bliss to walk in the scented moonlit garden with Sterling.

They came to a bench, and as Sterling sat, Sara sat

beside him. His hand left hers, and his arm went around her shoulders.

For a while they sat in silence. Sterling was so close to Sara that she could feel the hardness of his ribs against her. Closing her eyes, she leaned against him. *I'm happy,* she thought. *For once, I don't have to think about any of the things that usually haunt me, I can just savor this closeness with the man I love.*

She started when his voice broke the stillness. "Remember what I once told you?"

"Remind me."

"I want to show you what it's like to be a woman. What it's like for a man and a woman to enjoy each other." His voice was rough.

Desire heightened inside her. "Oh, that."

"Then you do remember?"

"Yes."

Stop talking, she wanted to tell him. *Just kiss me.*

A few seconds later, he did. With his arm still around her, he used his other hand to turn her toward him. He kissed her mouth and her cheeks, then her eyelids and her ears. Last of all, he brushed his tongue up and down her throat.

"Like that?" he asked.

"Not bad at all," she whispered.

"You were born to be loved, Sara." Again that rough voice, only rougher this time.

"You've said that before, too."

"I want you to understand."

Kiss me, an inner voice pleaded with him. *Stop talking and kiss me all night. Never stop.*

"You're always so frightened, Sara."

"Sterling…"

"Usually you can't even bear to be touched. It's not normal, this fear. Men and women do kiss, make love."

"I know," she murmured.

"Are you saying you really do understand?" His voice throbbed with sudden urgency.

"Yes."

"Sara!"

And then he was pulling her against him until she half-sat, half-lay on his lap with her back against his supporting arm. His kisses were no longer gentle. They were hard, passionate, exploring. Finally, they demanded a response from her. A response that she ached to give.

Sterling made a sound in his throat when Sara put her hands around his head and drew him closer, when her lips opened to his kisses and she kissed him with an abandon she had never thought possible.

When they drew apart at last, he said, "Sara! My God, Sara, this is… It's incredible!"

"Yes!"

"I want so much more from you, sweetheart. But I don't want to push you. We can take things slowly."

Slowly? When her own life was moving so quickly, when circumstances—the baby growing inside her, Emma's return—would soon drive her away from the man she'd grown to love? Slowness was the one luxury she could no longer afford.

The baby. She wanted so badly to make love with Sterling, but she could not do anything that would harm her baby.

And then she remembered the words of the doctor who had confirmed the pregnancy, telling her—among other things—that lovemaking was safe. "You'll be glad to know it," the smiling doctor had told her. "You and your partner can go on with your lives as usual." Sara, re-pulsed, had not told her that the very last thing she intended was to let Larry into her bed.

But Sterling wasn't Larry. And she wanted him so badly.

"You don't have to take anything slowly, Sterling." Her throat was tight with desire.

Sterling was staring at her in the darkness. Against her body, she could feel the throbbing of his desire, the tension of the hard muscles of his arms and thighs.

"I hope you know what you're saying." He ground the words out hoarsely. "If we don't stop now, I'll end up spending the night making love to you."

"I know."

"I don't understand, Sara." His voice was thick with disbelief. "Until today you didn't even want to be kissed. Now you're saying you'll let me make love to you?"

"Yes, Sterling. Yes!"

"Sara!" Her name emerged on a groan.

"Sterling... Sterling, let's not wait any longer."

"Am I dreaming?" he asked wonderingly. "Did you really say what I thought you said?"

"I did." Her lips were so dry that it was hard to speak.

She was about to move off his lap, but he moved before she did. In one second he was standing, bringing her up with him. And then he was carrying her into the house, kissing her as they went.

He did not put her down until they reached the bedroom. He switched on a lamp by his bed, bathing the room in soft light. Only then did he put her on the bed.

"Sterling." Sara looked at him with eyes that were wide and filled with love and pleading.

"Yes, Sara. My beautiful, lovely Sara." His voice was low, more tender than she had ever heard it.

And then they were kissing again. Kissing as if they could never get enough of each other.

"I'm going to undress you," he told her.

Slowly, infinitely seductively, he unbuttoned her blouse and slipped it from her shoulders, then opened her belt and let her step out of her skirt. Sara shivered when he removed her underwear, until at last she lay before him, quite naked.

"God, but you're beautiful!" he groaned. "The most beautiful woman in the whole world."

"Really?" Sara asked, so softly that she didn't know whether the word made it past her lips.

"Don't you know it?"

He kissed her lips, then his mouth moved lower, to her

throat, over her breasts where the nipples became hard peaks in seconds, over her stomach and her thighs.

"Undress me, too, sweetheart," he pleaded.

Sara did so, moving as slowly as he had, even though every nerve ending urged her to hurry. When Sterling was also naked she gazed at him, awed by the magnitude of his desire and by the awareness of what she had done to him.

Sterling lay on the bed beside her and gathered her to him. For a while they lay together, caressing, kissing, exploring, their desire increasing second by second to the point where it was no longer possible to delay the final fulfillment.

"Are you ready?" His voice was so deep, so intense that she barely recognized it.

"Oh, yes!" And then, thinking of the baby, "Be gentle, Sterling. Please, be gentle."

"Your first time, sweetheart." His voice was ragged. "I want it to be wonderful for you. I'd never hurt you."

Sara heard the words, but now was not the time for talking. Especially since he was kissing her again.

When at last he entered her, the lovemaking was everything Sara had hoped for. Exciting beyond all words, blissful beyond anything she had ever imagined. Not once with Larry had there been this explosion of sounds, of stars, this ecstasy that was like nothing else.

Afterward they lay together a long while, wrapped in an intimacy that needed no words. When Sterling did speak at last, he said, "That was... I don't have words to describe it."

"For me, too," she said softly.

"I was so anxious for you, Sara. I hoped I wouldn't hurt you."

"You didn't."

"I never dreamed it could be like this, Sara."

"I didn't know it, either," she whispered, and she was speaking the truth.

With Larry, it had been so different. There had been

none of the ecstasy she had just experienced. In the latter part of their relationship she had submitted to his love-making only because if she didn't, he made her suffer.

What had just happened had been more wonderful than she had ever imagined. Sterling had made it wonderful. She loved him even more now than before. Whatever the future held for her, one thing was certain. She would probably love him always.

"Hi, Sleeping Beauty."

As Sara opened her eyes, she was still filled with the delicious lassitude evoked by their lovemaking.

"Hi, yourself." She smiled into Sterling's face.

"Sleep well, Sara?"

"Never better." It was the truth. She had never been quite so blissfully happy as she was now.

Sterling bent and kissed her, his unshaven face sensuously rough against her soft skin. "Quite a night, Sara."

"It was," she agreed.

"You were so full of surprises, sweetheart."

"Really?"

"So passionate. In all my dreams—and I *have* dreamed about making love to you—I never expected such passion from you."

"Sterling," she began, knowing she could no longer keep him in ignorance of her sexual experience.

But Sterling cut in before she could go on. "And your body..."

"What about my body?" Sara was wary now.

"For someone so slender, there's a voluptuousness I never expected. Your breasts—" he stroked a nipple "—are so full. Even your tummy and your hips aren't quite as thin as I imagined. And yet the rest of you is so fragile. Your legs, your arms. Parts of you are so delicate, a man could think they'd snap in two if they were handled too roughly."

Sara's throat had a bitter taste suddenly. "Sterling, I really think you—"

"Your body and your passion weren't the only things I didn't expect, Sara."

"What are you saying?" She guessed what was coming, and she found it difficult to speak.

The eyes looking at her were intent, probing. "I was so certain you were a virgin, Sara. But it wasn't the first time for you, after all, was it?"

"Sterling—"

"There are things a man knows, feels. And a virgin doesn't make love the way you did."

If only he would stop talking, stop turning the lovely dream into a nightmare.

"Why didn't you tell me, Sara?"

She stared at him through a haze of anger. "I didn't have to!"

"Didn't you?"

"No! Are you going to tell me my sexual status had something to do with my suitability for the job?"

"Obviously not," Sterling said. "I just wonder why you didn't tell me. Sara, all this time you pretended you were so innocent. Last night. You could have said something then. Why didn't you?"

Despite the warm body so close to her, Sara was beginning to feel cold. "All these questions!" she exclaimed.

"I do have questions, yes." Something in his glance deepened. "Did somebody hurt you, Sara? Is that it? I've asked you before, but you've never given me any answers."

"I...I can't."

As if he hadn't heard her, Sterling persisted. "Looking back, there were so many clues. *Have* you been hurt, Sara?"

"Sterling—"

"I need to know, Sara. Don't you understand?"

The eyes searching hers were warm with tenderness. How quickly that expression would change if she told him what he wanted to know. It was the reason she had kept it from him all along. Sara swallowed hard over the bitter taste in her mouth.

"I understand that you're asking too many questions. I won't have it, Sterling! I told you that when I first agreed to come here. No questions. That hasn't changed."

"Everything has changed, Sara," Sterling said quietly.

"No!"

"Sara—"

"No, Sterling, no!"

One thing hadn't changed, never would change. If Sterling heard her story, he would be filled with pity, perhaps even contempt. Now more than ever, Sara could not bear the thought of that pity. Not from Sterling. Not from the man she loved so deeply.

"Talk to me, Sara," he said.

But Sara had had enough talk.

"No more questions," she told him, and jumped out of bed.

Momentarily, she was unaware of her nakedness. When she registered the fact, she grabbed a sheet and wrapped it quickly around her.

"So modest all at once." Sterling sounded impatient, his gentleness suddenly gone. "You're forgetting, I know exactly how you look under that sheet. I know every inch of your delectable body."

"That's fine, because you won't be seeing it again. Ever."

Sterling leaped out of bed, too. Unlike Sara, he made no effort to conceal his nakedness. In the moments before he pulled on shirt and pants, Sara saw the body that had given her such pleasure, the tanned limbs, the wide chest, the corded muscles. Her breath caught in her throat, and her heart beat painfully.

As the memory of the things she had said and done the night before came to her, Sara's cheeks grew hot.

"I hope you're not denying you enjoyed making love, Sara."

"How can I?" she asked in a low voice. "But I wish with all my heart it hadn't happened."

"Why, Sara? Why?" Unexpectedly, he was gentle again.

The gentleness was her undoing. She didn't want to talk, to explain. Not now, perhaps never.

Quickly, Sara pulled on her clothes. She was hurrying to the door when Sterling said, "Stay. You don't have to talk if you don't want to."

In Sara's haste to get away, she didn't hear the conciliatory words. She ran through the house and pushed open the front door. She wasn't looking as she ran down the steps to the drive.

She didn't see the bicycle racing down the long driveway. She cried out as it hit her, and she hit her head as she fell to the ground.

She didn't hear Manuel's frantic shout. *"Señorita! Señorita!"*

Nor was she aware of Sterling rushing out of the house and gathering her in his arms. She didn't hear his equally frantic words. "Sara! My darling! What have I done to you?"

CHAPTER EIGHT

SARA'S leg and foot ached.

When she tried to move, to get into a more comfortable position, there was an awkwardness that prevented her from shifting more than a few inches. She tried to sit up, but dizziness overwhelmed her, making her sink immediately against the pillow. Her head hurt. Come to think of it, there wasn't a part of her that didn't hurt.

For a while she lay quite still. Eyes closed—it was too much effort to open them—she tried to cope with the awful dizziness. Once she did open her eyes, and saw things she'd never seen before. But the dizzy feeling increased, and she closed her eyes.

"Don't fight it," an unfamiliar female voice said.

"Fight," Sara responded vaguely.

"Go back to sleep. It's the best thing for you right now."

Something pricked her arm, but the feeling was momentary. She was so groggy she kept her eyes closed. Nothing seemed to matter. Who was speaking? Even that didn't matter.

The next time Sara woke, two people were talking. The unfamiliar woman again and someone else. *Sterling.* Even through her pain and confusion, Sara felt a surge of happiness knowing he was there.

"Sterling!" she called to him. But perhaps his name didn't make it past her lips, for there was no response from the man she loved so much.

Instead, she heard him say, "How long will she be like this?"

"Hard to say," the woman answered. "We've given her a shot for the pain. It's knocked her out, and that's

' good. She surfaces now and then, but she'll probably be out of things a while longer.''

If Sterling answered, Sara didn't hear him, for she'd drifted off again.

The next time she woke, she was able to open her eyes. For several moments she wondered if she was dreaming, because her surroundings made no sense to her. She was in a room with bare white walls and no pictures—her room at the wine estate was pale lemon—and the curtains that wafted in the breeze from the open window were unfamiliar. The bed she lay in was strange, too.

She was certain she had heard Sterling talking. Where was he? And where was she?

The baby. Had something happened to the baby? Was that why she was here? Dear God, no! *Please let the baby be okay.*

Anxious, she tried to sit. She had to find out where she was, find out about the baby, find someone she could talk to. It was hard to sit up when her foot dragged strangely beneath her, but she tried. In the process, her hand struck something beside the bed, and something thudded to the ground.

A minute later someone appeared in the room. ''You're awake, Sara.''

The woman was wearing white, and she was smiling. Sara recognized her voice.

''Something fell.''

''Only a book, honey. How are you feeling?''

''A bit dizzy.''

''Well, that's to be expected,'' the woman said kindly. ''Where am I?''

''You're in the hospital, Sara.''

She gaped at the woman. ''Why? Where's Sterling? What happened?''

The woman, a nurse, Sara realized, smiled as she held up a hand. ''Slowly, now, honey, one thing at a time. You had a bit of an accident. You were knocked down. You hit your head on the ground and gave your right ankle a nasty sprain.''

So that was why it was so difficult to move her leg, why she could feel a bandage.

"Knocked down?" she asked slowly.

"Don't you remember?"

She did remember something, though not much. Only that something had crashed into her. A cry. No more than that.

"A bit. I think something hit me. I don't know what."

"A bicycle," the nurse said. "Seems you ran into the road. The bike was coming along, but you didn't see it."

"How about the baby?" she asked urgently.

A look of surprise crossed the nurse's face. "I don't know about a baby. From what I heard you were the only one involved."

"You don't understand. There's something I have to know! Are you sure you don't know what happened?"

"Just the basic facts, I'm afraid."

A little more memory was beginning to surface now. There had been a headlong dash from a house. An urgent need to get away. Why?

"Where is Sterling?" Sara asked.

"He went out for a while, but he'll be along shortly. He was keen to be here when you woke."

Sterling. More memory now. Lovemaking. Wonderful lovemaking, fulfilling beyond her wildest dreams. And then a dreadful anger. Why had she been so angry that she'd had to run out of Sterling's house? Why, when all she wanted was to be with him?

Think. But she couldn't remember more. Not now, anyway.

Just then, someone said, "So you're awake."

"Sterling!" She hadn't heard him come in, and she looked at him happily.

"Hello, Sara." Even through her joy, she noticed a coolness in his tone.

"Sara was just asking after you, Mr. Tayler," said the

nurse. "I told her you'd be along, and here you are. I'll look in on you again soon, honey. Bring you something cool to drink, take your temperature and your pulse."

"I'm not sick," Sara protested.

"No, but you've had quite a shock. Why don't you just lie back and let yourself be spoiled?"

With that the nurse left the room, and Sara was glad to see her go. Pleasant as the woman was, she longed to be alone with Sterling. But Sterling wouldn't be able to help her with the one question she needed answered.

"I'm so glad you're here," she said.

"Really?" Sterling sounded so stiff that Sara was startled.

"Sterling, what's wrong?"

"It's as the nurse told you. You were knocked down by a bicycle."

"Apart from that?"

Unable to meet the strange hostility in Sterling's eyes, Sara moved her gaze. For the first time, she noticed a small vase of flowers on a table near the window.

"Flowers! Oh, Sterling, thank you."

"They're from Manuel."

There was only one lot of flowers in the room. Nothing from Sterling. Not that Sara expected anything. She didn't. All the same, it was odd that it was Manuel, a young boy with very little money to spend, who had thought to give her flowers.

"Why did he give me flowers?"

"You don't know?" Still that stiff tone.

"No. I mean, he's a sweet guy, but still… Why would Manuel do this for me?"

"Then you don't know. It was Manuel who ran into you. He was on his bike when you ran out of the house."

Sara's hand went to her mouth. "Oh, my God! Poor Manuel, he must feel terrible."

"Worse than you can imagine. He blames himself for what happened."

Sterling's expression was hard and cold. If he had any sympathy for Sara, he had an odd way of showing it.

"I'm so sorry."

"It wasn't his fault. Is there nothing you remember, Sara?"

"I remember leaving your house."

"Leaving isn't the word for it. You raced out as if the devil was chasing you. Manuel never had a chance, but he blames himself nevertheless. Nothing I say seems to console him. If not for Manuel's carelessness, the poor *señorita* wouldn't have been hurt."

"I'll have to try and convince him it wasn't his fault. I will try, Sterling, the first chance I get."

And I have to find out about the baby.

"Good luck with Manuel," Sterling said unsympathetically.

Something was very wrong. This wasn't the man she had fallen in love with, the tough, strong man who could be both gentle and tender.

She longed for him to sit beside her, to take her hand, to kiss her. Instead, all he did was stare moodily at her from a distance.

"Something's on your mind," she said at last.

"How perceptive of you to have noticed," he mocked.

"What is it, Sterling?"

"I'm wondering," he said in that same mocking tone, "how much you remember of our night together."

"You mean our lovemaking?"

"Right."

"I know what we did."

"Remember enjoying it?"

Her cheeks flushed. "Yes."

"Even though," Sterling said, and his tone was even more mocking, "until last night you made out you couldn't bear the thought of sex?"

"What are you getting at, Sterling?"

"Just the idea of being touched or kissed was anathema to you."

Deep inside Sara, a muscle tightened. Unhappily, she looked at Sterling. "Why are you talking like this?"

"I thought we had a great evening. That our lovemaking was fantastic."

"It was wonderful," Sara whispered.

"So wonderful that you ran out of the house the moment I started asking you a few questions."

"Very personal questions," she said, as memory returned.

"Too personal?" he asked mockingly.

"Yes." She was silent, absorbing Sterling's anger while her eyes searched the hostile face. "Why are you dredging it all up again now?"

"Because I want to understand. The innocent virgin— or so I thought—unkissed and untouched and determined to remain so. And yet not a virgin at all, as I learned last night. I asked you whether there was a reason for your silence. Whether you'd been hurt. But you wouldn't tell me. I'm asking again. Was there something in your past that made you frightened?"

Sara turned her eyes away. "I didn't want to talk about myself last night. I don't now. Can't you take a hint, Sterling?"

"I believe you owe me some explanations, Sara."

"I don't owe you a damn thing."

His eyes, steel hard, were so penetrating that Sara felt as if he could see her innermost thoughts.

"There's nothing you want to tell me, Sara?" His voice was odd.

Sara hesitated. She remembered how she had tried to tell Sterling about Larry. When he had refused to be serious, she had made up her mind to tell him the next day. Now she was glad she hadn't. Despite the fact that she loved Sterling, she didn't owe it to him to bare her pain before him. Besides, this new Sterling was showing the kind of contempt she had feared from the beginning.

Quietly, she said, "I have nothing to tell you."

"Interesting," he drawled.

And what did he mean by that? Perhaps it was time for her to go on the offensive.

"I do have a question of my own, Sterling."

"Fire away."

"Why are you so hostile? I've done nothing to deserve it."

"You don't think so?"

"No. I'll tell you what I think, Sterling. I wasn't the virgin you believed me to be, and now your pride is hurt, and you're letting out your anger on me."

"Is that really what you think, Sara?"

"Yes."

"Then there's nothing more to say."

"You're right, there isn't. I don't want to go on with this, Sterling. I can't take any more. My head hurts. My ankle, too."

What she didn't tell him was that the ache in her heart was the worst pain of all. The new Sterling would be totally unsympathetic.

Something moved in the depths of his eyes, but the expression vanished before she could make anything of it.

"Poor Sara," he said sarcastically.

"You may as well go, Sterling."

"I was about to. Goodbye, Sara."

Without another word, he walked through the door.

Alone in the room, Sara gazed at the flowers Manuel had sent her. She couldn't remember being so unhappy since the day she had left Larry. Something had happened to upset Sterling, but she had no idea what it could be. If only she could think. But her aching head made it difficult.

And yet she did have to think—about the baby. Had the fall done anything to harm her pregnancy? If only the baby was okay. The nurse didn't seem to know, but there had to be someone she could ask.

She was trying to sleep when a woman walked into the room, a stethoscope around her neck.

"I'm Dr. Madison," she introduced herself. "I attended to you when you were brought here."

"I don't remember."

"You wouldn't, Sara, you weren't aware of anything much at the time. I guess you know that you hit your head when you fell?" Sara nodded. "No damage, fortunately. No concussion, just enough of a jolt to give you a mammoth headache. And then there's your ankle. It's badly sprained. It will be a couple of weeks before you can walk comfortably again." She glanced at a chart by the bed, then went on. "I'd like to keep you here overnight for observation and to make certain nothing is going on that we don't know about. After that you can leave the hospital."

"Dr. Madison," Sara said anxiously. "I'm pregnant, and I need to know—is my baby okay?"

The doctor smiled at her. "I was about to mention the baby. It's fine, Sara."

"Thank God! I was so worried."

"I can imagine, but I thought you'd have heard already."

"The nurse didn't seem to know anything."

The doctor looked surprised. "She didn't, but I thought Mr. Tayler would have told you. Well, never mind. The good news, Sara, is that your fall didn't harm the baby."

She didn't seem to notice that Sara looked dazed.

"No risk of a miscarriage that I can see. Your baby is doing just fine, Sara. Nothing there for you to worry about."

"You told Sterling?"

"You were out of things at the time, and I thought you'd both want to know."

"Yes. Yes, I see."

The doctor was frowning. "I take it I didn't overstep the limits of doctor-patient confidentiality? Mr. Tayler was so distraught when he brought you in. The man is obviously deeply concerned about you. I thought I should at least put his mind at rest on the pregnancy issue."

"Yes."

"Any questions before I go, Sara?"

"No. Nothing. Thank you."

"I'll stop by and check on you again tomorrow. If everything is all right, you'll be able to leave then. In the meanwhile, rest as much as you can, Sara."

But there would be no rest for her now, Sara knew. Despite her throbbing head, she stared unseeingly at the wall in front of her.

Sterling knew she was pregnant. And he had decided to judge her accordingly. How dare he! How dare Sterling sit in judgment of her!

Her hands folded protectively over her stomach. *My darling baby,* she thought. *Nobody will humiliate you, I won't allow it. I'll give you a sense of pride in yourself, a knowledge that you are your own person, that you owe no explanations to anybody. It won't matter that you don't have a father because I'll do whatever is necessary to make you feel cherished. I'll love you and protect you, and we'll make a good life for ourselves, just the two of us.*

"Ready?" Sterling asked when he walked into the room the next day.

Her cheeks grew hot at his curtness. "Ready for what, exactly?"

"I've come to take you home."

"Your estate is not my home, Sterling. And I'm going nowhere with you."

His eyebrows rose. "I've been told you suffered no head injuries. Am I to take it you have, in fact, lost your mind?"

Scornfully, Sara said, "Do you know how pompous you sound when you talk that way? For your information, I've never been more fully in possession of my mind than right now. I'm not going with you, Sterling."

"Is there a reason?"

"You can bet your sweet life there is! You were told

something about me, and you condemned me on the strength of it.''

Sterling's face was autocratically stern. "So you know about that.''

"I do. I'm surprised you didn't ask me about the baby. I had to hear that you knew about it from Dr. Madison.''

"You're the right one to talk,'' Sterling responded stormily. "You had a few weeks to talk, but you didn't.''

She met the fierce look with one just as fierce. "Do you want to talk now?''

"In a hospital ward, where anyone can walk in at any moment? I think not, Sara. We'll do our talking at the estate.''

"In that case, we won't talk at all. Didn't you hear me the first time? I'm not going with you, Sterling. So will you please leave my room? I have some important decisions to make, and I need to think quickly.''

"You're a damn fool, Sara,'' he said savagely.

"You're welcome to think what you like. You do anyway, Sterling.''

"You're coming with me, so stop playing hard to get.''

"Is that what you think I'm doing?''

"We both know it.''

"Why would I even consider going with a man who treats me as if I'm dirt?''

The look he gave her was hard and bleak, with no hint of softening. "You'll come,'' he said flatly, "because you have a badly sprained ankle and nowhere else to go.''

"I'm not that desperate. I'll find a place.''

"Where, Sara? How?''

Questions she could not answer, no matter how angry she was. Blinking back tears, Sara gave him a defiant look. "That's my problem. I'll deal with it.''

"It's my problem, too,'' he told her. "The accident happened while you were in my employ.''

"Don't let it upset you.''

"Who said anything about being upset?'' Sterling countered smoothly.

"Well, then, don't feel responsible for me."

His answer was unexpected. "You're the one who should be feeling responsible. Have you forgotten your commitment? Emma won't be back until the end of next month. You have work to do until then."

"With a sprained ankle?" Sara asked caustically. "The doctor said it will be a couple of weeks before I can get around properly."

"You don't do office work with your ankle, and there's nothing wrong with your hands. According to you, there's nothing wrong with your head, either, so there's absolutely no reason why you shouldn't be able to work a computer." His tone was as caustic as hers.

Sara acknowledged a sense of relief—though she would not let Sterling know it. When he had come barging into her room, she hadn't decided where to go. She could have thrown herself on Paula's friendship. The waitress might have let her stay until Sara found another job. But that was a last-resort solution. Paula might regret her impulsive offer yet be too kind to say so. Although Sara hated the idea of returning to the wine estate with Sterling, it was probably the best solution.

She sighed. "You win. I'll go with you. And I'll leave the moment Emma gets back."

Sterling shrugged. "Can you get dressed or do you need help?"

The last time they had been together there had been such a sensuous joy in their undressing of each other. Hard to believe their wonderful lovemaking had taken place so recently.

"I'll manage on my own, thanks. If you'll leave the room, that is. I don't care to be watched."

"Such modesty," Sterling said, sneering. "And to think I was taken in by it. You're a great actress, Sara."

"Get out!" she said angrily.

"How many men have seen you naked, Sara?"

Oh, but this was too much! Without thinking, she

picked up the glass beside her bed and threw the water at him, splashing his face and his shirt.

He seized her wrists. "So this is the real Sara." He bit the words out. "Not the sweet innocent, after all, but the savage vixen."

"You're welcome to your opinion," she taunted, and wished his hands weren't so madly exciting.

"I have more than one opinion of you, Sara," Sterling said roughly. "Some of them not very flattering."

"I'll bet they're not! Look, Sterling, why don't we just call it quits? I haven't forgotten the commitment, and I'll honor it if you really want me to, but I still think you could find yourself some other secretary, and I'll make my own arrangements."

"I'm holding you to your word, Sara, like it or not. Now, are you going to dress yourself or am I going to do it for you? Either way, I intend leaving this place in the next ten minutes."

"I'll be ready," she said flatly.

Sara sat stiffly on the way to the wine estate, blinking back tears as she stared unseeingly out the front window. Now and then Sterling glanced her way. In spite of the painkiller she had taken shortly before leaving the hospital, her ankle ached, but she wouldn't give him the satisfaction of admitting it.

"Can you walk?" he asked as he stopped the car.

He had transported her in a wheelchair from the hospital building to the parking lot. Sara had been given crutches and instructions on how to use them but hadn't had much chance to try them. Apprehensively, she eyed the steps that led to the front door of her house.

Sterling must have followed the direction of her eyes. Without a word he scooped her into his arms and carried her inside.

Briefly, Sara closed her eyes, remembering the passion she had sensed in Sterling's body two days earlier when he had carried her to his bedroom. There was nothing even remotely lover-like about him now. She opened her eyes when he put her on her bed and said, "Thanks."

"I'll bring your crutches. That way you'll be able to get around the house."

"Yes. Thanks."

He looked at her. "Though perhaps you should stay in the big house until you're sure of your mobility."

Sara's answer was quick and unhesitating. "I wouldn't think of it."

"If that's the way you feel about it." He paused before adding, "If you need something, use the phone and call me."

Stiffly, Sara said, "I'm sure that won't be necessary."

For the first time that day, Sterling grinned. "It's always a mistake to box yourself into a corner, Sara. Makes it difficult to leave the corner when you want to. I may have some rather strong feelings about you, but it doesn't mean I'd leave you helpless. I wouldn't let you starve or rot."

"How charmingly put, Sterling." Despite herself, Sara found herself grinning at him. "You're more gallant than I gave you credit for."

Manuel came to see her an hour later. When Sara had thanked him for the flowers, he said, "I cannot forgive myself, *señorita.*"

"It wasn't your fault, Manuel," Sara said contritely. "According to Sterling, I ran into the road without looking. I should have seen you, but I didn't."

"You were in a hurry," Manuel acknowledged, "but that doesn't excuse what I did. I was beside myself when you fell. And so was the boss."

"Sterling was upset?" she asked curiously.

"Upset is not the word for it, *señorita.* He was out of his mind, that man. I think he cares for you very much."

The words gave Sara a few seconds of pleasure. Until she remembered that any emotion Sterling might have shown had been before he'd learned about her pregnancy. It was only afterward that the awful hostility had set in.

"Can I do something, for you, *señorita?*"

"No thanks, Manuel. I'm a little tired. What I really need right now is to sleep. Thanks again for the beautiful flowers."

"You're awake."

Sara turned her head on the pillow. "Yes."

When Sterling had carried her into the house, the room had been bathed in the brightness of noon sunlight. It was almost dark now.

"Have I been sleeping all this time?"

"Several hours," Sterling said in the brusque tone that was become so horribly familiar. "There's some supper for you in the kitchen. I'll go and warm it in the microwave."

"I'm not very hungry."

"Haven't I heard that before? Seems to me you haven't been very hungry—" the last two words were spoken with jeering emphasis "—since the first day we met. At the time I put it down to your being upset at the way you'd been treated in the diner. Now, of course, I know there was a different reason."

Sara threw him a steady look. "Quite right, there was."

"Don't pregnant women normally eat for two?"

"Since this is the first time I've been pregnant, I don't know much about it yet."

"At least you're not denying it." The look he treated her to was contemptuous in the extreme.

Sara moved her eyes. Although she had to stand firm in the face of Sterling's hostility, it hurt to see how much he despised her.

"Of course, I'm not denying it," she said firmly.

"Judging by your manner, I'd say you're proud of it."

Sara's head jerked in Sterling's direction. "I'm certainly not ashamed."

"Then why, may I ask, did you say you were a virgin?"

"I never said it."

"Give me a break!" Sterling growled.

"But I didn't. Not once. What I said was that I was averse to sex."

"I believed you were a virgin." Sterling was clearly outraged. "Whenever I tried to touch you or kiss you, you behaved like a frightened rabbit."

"From which you drew your conclusions. The wrong ones, as it happened."

"I know that now. But you knew they were wrong, Sara, and yet you did nothing to correct me. Why not?"

"There was a reason," she said quietly.

Dark eyes searched her face. "I believe there was," he said at last.

Sara found it hard to meet his gaze. When Sterling said, "Do you want to tell me about it?" she looked away.

For a moment she was tempted to talk to Sterling. Then she remembered once more that she could not bear his pity and contempt. That had not changed, would never change.

Flatly, she said, "Surely you must realize by now that I don't."

His expression grew hard. "You were so shy, so innocent. God, Sara, when I think how I was taken in by your dishonesty, I see red. I wanted so much to make love to you, but I thought I had to give you time, take things slowly."

"Yes."

"I was willing to do things your way. Do you know why?"

"No." She wasn't sure why she was trembling.

"I was falling in love with you, Sara."

"You were?"

"There—I thought that would shock you."

Incredulously, Sara stared at Sterling. Joy rushed through her, a joy that was pure and simple and all-encompassing, pulsing in her veins, making her heart beat wildly. *Sterling loved her.* Her lips parted. She was about to tell him that she loved him, too.

And then she saw his expression. Sterling's eyes were

hard. His jaw was like steel. The only emotion in his face was dislike. At that moment Sara realized that when he'd talked about love, he had used the past tense. Any feelings Sterling had once had for her were dead. That being the case, it would be useless to tell him of her feelings.

"What shocks me is that you judged me," she said harshly.

"Oh, really," he said mockingly.

"There's no shame in being a single mother. A single woman has just as much right to her baby as anyone else. And for your information, I'll love my child as deeply as if I were married. I love it already, Sterling. And I won't have any stigma attached to myself or to my baby. Not now, not ever."

"Quite a speech, Sara." The look he threw her was scathing. "You haven't mentioned the father."

She felt cold suddenly. "No."

"Where is he?"

"That doesn't concern you."

"Who is he?"

"Doesn't concern you, either."

Moodily, restlessly, Sterling paced the room. He was like a huge caged animal, Sara thought, a lion or a panther, a predator accustomed to roaming the bush, uncomfortable when it was restrained.

Suddenly he stood still. "Larry!" He flung the name at her.

The blood drained from Sara's cheeks. She should have expected Sterling to make the deduction, but oddly she hadn't, perhaps because she hadn't been able to focus on very much since the accident.

"You had a dream once about a man called Larry."

"A *dream*, Sterling. I told you at the time not to make a big deal of it."

"We both know it was more than a dream. Is he the father? He is, Sara, isn't he?"

She tried very hard to keep her face expressionless. "The father's identity isn't important."

"Is it Larry?"

"I don't want to talk about this any longer."

Sterling covered the distance to the bed in one stride. "Tell me, Sara! You owe me that much."

"I don't owe you anything," she said shakily.

But she did owe him something, she knew that. But for Sterling, Sara would still be working in the diner, suffering the rudeness of the customers, struggling to find a way to save enough money to provide a few essentials for herself and the baby. Sterling had rescued her from all that. In the process, she had not only fallen in love with him but was now going to break her heart over him, as well.

"Tell me," he insisted.

"Leave me alone," she ordered.

"Sara!"

He was bending over her, so close to her that his breath heated her face. His tension communicated itself to every nerve of her body.

"I can't talk like this," she whispered.

Abruptly, Sterling took a step away from the bed. "Tell me."

"Larry is the father," Sara said.

Something moved in Sterling's jaw, but the rest of his face remained hard. When he spoke his voice was quiet and very dangerous. "You could have said so at the start."

"No."

"You'd have saved me a lot of..." He stopped.

"Of?" Sara prompted, a little breathlessly.

"It doesn't matter. Not now." Not a trace of softening in his tone, not even the slightest hint of affection.

He hates me, Sara thought.

Several seconds passed. They were both breathing harshly. There was no other sound.

"I'd like you to leave now," Sara said.

"The phrase you fall back on whenever you don't feel like facing facts. I'm not ready to leave, Sara. Not yet."

"I've already told you I don't feel like talking."

"Too bad, because I want to know about Larry."

Her heart thudded painfully. "No, Sterling."

"Yes, damn you. I want to know. I have to!"

Sara stared at him a long moment. Her expression might be cool, but she was a raw mass of pain. "What can I tell you, Sterling? Larry is an executive in a large company."

"Where?"

"In Maine."

"Are you married to him?" he demanded. "Is that why you've been holding out on me? Because all the time you belonged to someone else?"

He seemed to be waiting quite intensely for her answer.

"I've never been married." Deliberately, she added, "And I don't belong to anyone. I never will."

Sterling let the remark pass. He asked, "Was it a one-night stand?"

She wanted so badly to say yes, but she had to be honest with him. "No, it was a lot more than that."

His expression was more contemptuous than she had ever seen it. "So you actually carried on a relationship with this man?" the hostile Sterling asked.

Once again, he was going too far, demanding to know things that were none of his business. Sara loved Sterling passionately, but she had no intention of letting herself be intimidated by his insufferable attitude.

"Larry and I had a relationship." Angrily, she hurled the words at him. "We lived together. We were together a few months. That's what you want to know, isn't it, Sterling? And now you think the worst of me. I see it in your eyes."

"You disgust me," he said savagely.

The breath was hot in her throat, threatening to choke her.

"Does my disgust shock you, Sara?" he asked.

When she could speak, she said, "Yes, it does. I took you for a tolerant man, Sterling. A man who wouldn't make snap judgments. A person who would understand that in today's world there are thousands upon thousands of single mothers. And children who deserve as much love as those born to married couples.''

''I'm not judging your child,'' he said harshly. ''My contempt is solely for you. Why didn't you tell me the truth?''

''I was going to.''

''Easy to say that now,'' he taunted.

''The evening we made love—I told you there was something I needed to tell you.''

Sterling frowned. ''So you did.''

''You didn't want to hear what I had to say. I tried more than once. You asked me a lot of funny questions. You weren't in the mood for serious talk.''

''That's right, I wasn't. That night was a time for loving.'' He paused, then corrected himself. ''For *sex*.''

Sara felt tears gather, but she managed to blink them back. She would not give Sterling the satisfaction of seeing her cry.

Unsteadily, she said, ''You like to pour salt in the wounds, Sterling.''

''Do I?'' he jeered.

She nodded.

''At any rate, there came a time,'' Sterling said, ''when I did give you a chance to talk. By then you had changed your mind.''

''I thought the facts would keep a few hours, that I'd tell you the next day. I couldn't have known there'd be an accident.''

''You couldn't,'' he conceded. ''But you could have told me long before, Sara. You didn't. You decided to hide your pregnancy. Until two days ago, you had no intention of telling me the truth.''

The truth. She had intended telling Sterling everything, about the pregnancy, about the abuse and the blackmail and Larry's appalling behavior when he had learned about the baby.

But Sterling didn't deserve the truth. Not any longer. His contempt at learning that she was unmarried and pregnant made it impossible to talk openly. More than that, she no longer wanted to. Sterling was not, after all, the man she'd begun to think him to be. Just as well she had learned that before she made a total fool of herself.

If only she hadn't allowed herself to fall in love with him, she wouldn't be feeling quite so devastated.

"Why aren't you with your Larry now?"

Her Larry? The words made Sara shudder with revulsion.

She shrugged. "Circumstances."

"Will you go back to him when the baby is born?"

"That's a long way off, and I don't want to discuss the future."

"A father deserves to know his child."

Not Larry. Not the man who had punched her in the stomach hoping she would lose the baby. The man who had ordered her to have an abortion.

"I told you, Sterling, I don't want to discuss it."

If only he would go, Sara thought. She had had about as much as she could take for one day. She needed to be alone, to think, to weep.

But Sterling stood there looking at her. "One more question, Sara."

"Why do I get the feeling it's loaded?"

"Do you love Larry?"

Sara flinched. "What kind of question is that?"

"A simple one. Do you love him?"

Simple? Oh, no, Sterling, she thought, *it's not simple at all. If I told you the whole awful story, there'd be a slew of new questions. I intended to tell you about Larry, but now I can't.*

In the end, there was only one way to answer him. "I wouldn't have gone to live with Larry if I hadn't thought I loved him." Sterling didn't hear the words she added silently. *At the time.*

His expression changed. The contempt was gone. In its place was something far worse. Sara saw it but did not understand it. She suppressed a shiver.

He was opening his mouth to speak, but Sara got in first.

"No more talking, Sterling. I'm not up to it. And forget about the food you were going to warm for me, because I couldn't eat it."

"Sara…"

"I'm exhausted, Sterling. I need to be alone now. Please…please understand."

CHAPTER NINE

"SOMEONE to see you, Sara."

She lifted her eyes from the computer screen. "To see me?"

"That's what I said."

"Who?" Sara asked, but even as she spoke, a knot of tension formed in the pit of her stomach. "Nobody knows I'm here."

"This person obviously does." There was steel in Sterling's voice.

No! she thought wildly. *Oh, God, no!*

Three days had passed since her return from the hospital. Larry had not been mentioned once in that time. It was as if the heated argument had left Sara and Sterling drained and unready for more verbal combat.

They had managed to settle into a routine of a kind. After the first day, Sara had returned to her office. A certain amount of correspondence and accounts had piled up in her absence, but the responsibilities of the office were a relief, allowing her the luxury of concentrating on something other than her own problems.

Any conversation was impersonal and related to work. Sara hadn't forgiven Sterling for his audacity in condemning her pregnancy. Sterling clearly hadn't forgiven her for not telling him the truth. So they avoided the topics that were uppermost in both their minds.

One thing had not changed. Sara's love for Sterling was as deep and as passionate as ever. At night, when she remembered that each passing day brought her departure from the wine estate closer, she experienced pure agony.

All this was forgotten as she stared at Sterling. "Who...who is it?"

"A man."

"Not…" She was unable to say the name.

"Larry, that's right. Your dearly beloved Larry. In person."

"My God! Where is he?" Her throat was so dry that the words barely made it past her lips.

"I told him he could park his car around the back. He knows where you are."

"No!" *He can't come in here.*

"Sara?"

She did not hear the surprise in Sterling's voice. All she knew was that she could not let Larry find her. Could not bear to see him or talk to him. Without thinking, intent only on getting out of the office, she leaped from her chair.

Sterling caught her as the injured ankle gave way beneath her. "Sara! Sara, are you okay?" His voice had changed as he lifted her into his arms.

The warmth of his body set instant fire to her fevered nerves, but now was not the time to think about it.

"Help me!" she cried wildly.

"What do you want me to do?"

"Take me to my room. No! Not there! Maybe to—"

"Sara. Sara, you're trembling."

Sterling cradled her closer, and despite her need to escape she gave in to the temptation to lean her face against him. It was so long since she had been close to him.

"Put her down!"

Sterling wheeled as Sara lifted a horrified face.

"Larry," she said in a strangled voice.

"Did you hear me?" Larry raged.

The hostile tone must have got to Sterling. "I didn't hear Sara asking to be put down," he said coldly.

"Don't leave me," she whispered in his ear.

"Put my woman down! And then get yourself out of here!" Arrogant commands.

Sara found her voice. "Sterling is going nowhere. How did you find me, Larry?"

"Someone called me. Guy called Albert. Claimed a reward I'd been offering. Told me where to find my woman.''

''Albert?'' Sterling sounded surprised. ''How would he know about this man? I don't understand.''

Sara explained quickly. ''There was an ad in one of the Maine papers. Albert must have seen it.''

''Right,'' Larry said.

''Will someone please tell me what this is all about?'' Sterling asked.

''I told you to put down my woman,'' Larry snapped.

''I'm not your woman, Larry,'' Sara said as firmly as she could. ''And I want you to go.''

She felt ill as she took in the man who had once been so important to her. Beneath the superficial good looks, she saw the bully-boy twist of his lips, the nastiness in his narrow eyes, the weak chin. His face revealed the inherent cruelty of a man who thought nothing of hurting a woman. How was it possible that she could have been blind to his true character for so long?

''I'm not leaving without you, Sara,'' Larry said furiously. ''I warned you I'd never let you get away from me, and I meant it. Put her down, Tayler. The woman knows I won't permit another man to put his hands on her.''

''Go!'' Sara's tone was anguished.

Larry grabbed her arm, hurting her as he tried to pull her away from Sterling. She cried out, and Sterling said, ''Careful, man! Her ankle is badly sprained. If she falls she'll hurt herself, to say nothing of the baby.''

''Baby?'' Larry took a step backward. ''What baby? Didn't you have an abortion, Sara? I ordered you to.''

''I don't take orders, Larry. Not anymore.''

''You'll damn well get rid of this baby. You know how I feel about it.''

''I'm going to have the baby, Larry. Now leave! Immediately!''

''With you, Sara. You'll come with me, or I won't answer for the consequences.''

''Don't you dare talk to her like that,'' Sterling warned.

"I'll talk to her any way I damn well like. Get out of my way, Tayler."

"Don't leave me, Sterling!" Sara pleaded.

"I don't pretend to understand what's happening, but I wouldn't leave you if my life depended on it." Sterling was still holding her.

Larry grabbed her again.

"No!" Sara exploded. "I'm not coming with you, Larry. You'll never abuse me again! It's over, don't you understand?"

His fingers bit into her arm. "I understand that you're my woman. That you're carrying my baby."

"A baby you don't want. A baby you tried to kill when you punched my stomach."

Larry was opening his mouth to retort when Sterling said, very quietly, "A baby that will be mine."

Both heads jerked to him.

"I don't think I heard you right, Tayler." Larry's tone was menacing.

"Then I'll say it again. That baby is going to be mine. You see, Sara and I are engaged to be married."

Sara gasped.

Larry said, "In your dreams, Tayler. You'll never marry my woman."

"You're the one who's wrong, mister. Now listen very carefully, because I'm not going to repeat myself. The baby will be born after our marriage, and I intend adopting it. I will be the father of Sara's baby."

"I'll fight you on this."

"Go ahead." Sterling was unperturbed.

"I'll hire the best lawyers. Nobody will let you take this woman or the baby. Money is no object."

"I can afford lawyers, too," Sterling said briskly. "Go to court if you like, but I'm telling you now, you don't have a chance."

"You're not going to let him do this, Sara." Larry's tone was blustering, a tone Sara remembered from their last weeks together.

"You heard what Sterling said," she told him.

"You're not really engaged. You wouldn't marry a man like this. A farmer." The last two words were spoken with deliberate scorn.

Little did Larry know that she would jump at the chance. Of course, Sara knew that Sterling was pretending, that he had recognized the situation and was giving her a way out. But Larry was not to know it.

"You heard him, Larry," she said, as Sterling drew her closer.

Larry stared at her, his face an ugly mask of frustration. "There's something you're forgetting."

"I don't believe there is." But her heart sank in anticipation of the threat he was going to make.

"Your father," Larry drawled maliciously. "You're forgetting his job with the company. He'll be out on his ear the moment I get back to Maine."

"Don't do this, Larry."

"Thirty years, is it? Poor old Dad badly wants to make it to thirty-five so he can collect a decent pension. As you know, my dear Sara."

"Sounds like blackmail." Sterling's tone was thick with distaste.

"Call it what you like, Tayler. Sara always knew the score, didn't you, girl?"

"It's the only reason I stayed with you as long as I did," she told him. "The reason I suffered your abuse, mental as well as physical. If it hadn't been for my father, I'd have left you long before I did."

"And now you'll come back for the same reason."

"She will not," Sterling said. "You forget, Sara is going to be my wife."

At almost the same moment, Sara said, "I'm not going back to you, Larry. Ever. It's over, don't you understand?"

"I just hope your father understands when he's out on the street."

That was the moment Sara almost gave in to him.

Faintly, she said, "Dad wouldn't want me to suffer. He'd be furious if he knew what I've already put up with for his sake."

"You're quite right, your father won't suffer," Sterling said. "I don't know exactly what this is all about, although I think I'm getting a pretty fair idea. Thirty years entitles any man to keep his job and his pension. If you try any dirty tricks, Larry, my lawyers will take you on—and win. Further than that, if your father wants to go on working, Sara, and if he doesn't want to continue in his present work, I can always find a place for a good man."

"Words," Larry said with a sneer, but Sara saw that he wasn't looking quite as sure of himself.

"Words that I happen to be getting mighty tired of," Sterling told him. "Sara asked you to leave. Now I'm ordering you to get out."

"You can't force me." Larry's tone was belligerent.

Sterling put Sara gently on her typing chair. Then he turned to Larry. "This is my place, and I can force you. Easily. And rearrange your ugly face in the process. Is that what you want? Or will you go of your own free will?"

Sara held her breath as Larry looked at Sterling. She could see that Larry was flexing his arm muscles, as if in preparation for a fight.

"What's it to be?" Sterling asked very quietly, and Sara wondered whether Larry heard the fury and the danger in his tone.

Larry took a step forward, one hand lifting in a fist. But as if he knew he didn't stand a chance in a tangle with Sterling, he retreated.

"I'll go," he said resentfully.

"Thought you would."

"Not that I'm scared of a fight—I could beat you with one finger, Tayler. Just that I wouldn't demean myself by getting into a brawl with someone like you."

"Whatever you say," Sterling responded politely.

"You'll regret this, Sara."

"I will not," she said.

"*You* will regret it if you're not out of here in thirty seconds." Sterling's tone made it clear that he meant what he said.

Larry left with a vicious glance at Sara. Minutes later, they heard the sound of his car speeding away from the big house.

"Thank you," Sara said.

With Larry gone and the drama of his threats resolved, she felt drained.

"Nothing to thank me for."

She closed her eyes, willing the tension to leave her body, forcing her shallow breathing to return to normal. When she opened her eyes, she saw Sterling leaning against the desk not two feet from her, watching her intently.

Faintly, she said, "You saved me from a very nasty situation."

"I couldn't let you go back to a man like that. How did he know where to find you? Something about an advertisement, I think he said."

"He advertised in the local Maine papers. Offered a sizable reward. I spotted the ad in the library a few days ago."

"You were upset when you returned from town, I remember."

"With good reason. I realized from what Albert said that day in the wineries that he must have read something about me."

"The ad?"

"An article, probably," Sara said thoughtfully. "Larry has clout with the media, and I believe he got them to print something about me. I imagine the ad came after that."

"How big was the reward?"

Sara met his eyes. "A thousand dollars."

Sterling whistled. "Valuable woman! I'm impressed."

"So you should be." With Larry gone, it was easy to tease.

"About Albert, Sara..."

"He was so certain he knew me, Sterling. He must have gone to the Maine papers to find out more about me. It wouldn't have taken him long to find the ad."

"Did he strike you as a man who was hard up?"

"He was a man who wanted revenge. I hurt his pride when I slapped him. You were right about one thing, Sterling, I'll have to develop different techniques for dealing with creeps."

"What intrigues me," said the man she loved, "is that I was right all along—you really were a woman on the run." His eyes were sparkling with amusement.

"Did you think I was in trouble with the law, Sterling? Even though I told you I wasn't?"

The smile left his face. "Not once. Something was very wrong, but right from the start, I knew it wasn't anything you'd done."

Silence fell between them then, and Sara felt suddenly awkward. She knew the topic that was on both their minds, knew the sooner they spoke about it the better.

"Sterling," she began.

"Yes, Sara?" he drawled.

"About the engagement..."

"What about it, my darling?"

Her head whirled. When it settled safely on her neck, she said, "Don't call me that."

"Isn't that what people usually call their fiancées?" He stepped closer, trailed a sensuous finger around her lips, then bent and kissed her.

Oh, but he was making this difficult for her. "But I'm not your fiancée."

"Aren't you, my darling?"

That word again! She shot him a quick glance. "I appreciate what you did for me. Telling Larry we were going to be married. It worked. He believed you, even though he pretended he didn't."

"Why shouldn't he?"

"No reason, I suppose. But, Sterling, the whole thing was an act. We both know that. I mean, we're not really getting married."

"We're not?"

"Stop teasing, Sterling! You don't really have any intention of being my baby's father. Larry's gone, so you can drop the act now."

"Act, darling?" Once more he kissed her.

Inside Sara, desire was springing to vivid life. If Sterling were to carry her to bed and make love to her, she would not be able to resist him, even with a sprained ankle. That was why she had to stop him before the nonsense got completely out of hand.

"We both know it was an act," she said with all the firmness she could muster.

"Do we?"

"How could it be anything else when all you feel for me is contempt?"

"Actually," Sterling said softly, "all I feel for you is love."

"I don't believe you!" Sara was trembling.

"You should. I've always loved you, my darling."

"Why didn't you tell me?"

"You made it difficult for me, Sara. You were so scared, or so I thought. You didn't want to be touched, kissed. I felt I had to go slowly."

"I really was scared," she admitted. "That never was an act, Sterling."

"Because of Larry?"

Sara nodded. "Sterling, try and understand. At the beginning of our relationship, things were so different. Larry was charming, persuasive. I'd never met anyone like him. I thought I loved him—though I realize I never did. And then he abused me."

Sterling's eyes were hard with anger. Just as well Larry was gone, Sara thought, because there was no knowing what Sterling might do to him.

He said, "You didn't think of leaving him as soon as it started?"

"I did, many times. But he made me believe I was responsible for the abuse. And there were the threats to my father. Blackmail, just as you said."

"Why did you give in, Sara?"

"My parents haven't had an easy life. Dad's job means a lot to him. I couldn't let him lose everything because of me."

"Larry won't have your father fired. That's all bluster." Sterling spoke with quiet certainty. "He's a bully and a weakling, but that kind of man doesn't do the things he threatens. In any event, I meant what I said, Sara. There will be a job here for your father any time he wants it."

"You don't know what that means to me."

He lifted her out of her chair, then sat in it with Sara on his lap. Beneath her legs, his thighs were superbly hard and muscled. Sara leaned her head against him, reveling in the feel of his throat against her cheek. She closed her eyes as she felt Sterling's lips move in her hair.

After a while, Sterling said, "But you did leave him."

"I told Larry about the pregnancy. He was furious. Out of control. A lot of this you know already from what was said. He ordered me to have an abortion. When I refused, he hurt me. It was obvious he wanted me to lose the baby. That's when I knew I couldn't stay. I hoped with all my heart that nothing would happen to Dad, but I knew that for the sake of the baby—and myself—I had to go. I fled Maine and came to the one place where I didn't think Larry would ever find me. It never occurred to me that he would resort to advertising."

"About your fear of sex, darling…"

"I was so frightened. I didn't know how I could ever trust another man. I didn't want to let myself get close to a man again."

"That explains a lot," Sterling said thoughtfully.

"At the same time," she said, "I was falling in love with you."

"Sara!" Her name emerged in a joyful shout. "Did you really say that?"

"I didn't want it to happen, but it did. A very different emotion from the infatuation I felt for Larry. The kind of love I never imagined was possible."

"Oh, Sara! My darling Sara!"

He turned her in his lap so he could kiss her.

After a while, he said, "Why didn't you tell me about the abuse and the blackmail?"

"I couldn't."

"Why not? Surely you weren't ashamed? You had nothing to be ashamed of, darling."

"I didn't want your pity," she said slowly.

"Pity!"

"I saw pity in other people. People who saw my face before the bruises faded and who didn't believe my stories about accidents. It was awful, Sterling. I couldn't bear to see that pity in your eyes."

"I think I understand."

"Pity and contempt. I thought you'd be really contemptuous that I'd stuck it out for so long."

"I wish you had told me, Sara. If only…" He stopped. "The mark on your arm. That was from Larry?"

"He hit me with a broken bottle."

"I should have beaten him to a pulp," Sterling said fiercely.

"Oh, darling." Sara laughed with a sob as she used the endearment for the first time. "I wouldn't have wanted that. I'd have felt sick if there'd been a fight. You got Larry to leave, that's all that matters to me. I don't need revenge."

They sat quietly, kissing, caressing. Feeling the strength of the man who held her, strength that was both physical and mental, reveling in the sexiness that clung to him like a second skin, Sara knew she had never been so happy.

Presently, Sterling said, "I understand why you didn't tell me about the abuse and the blackmail. But how about the pregnancy?"

The words were like cold water dashed without warning over her face. "Do we have to talk about it?"

"You know we do, Sara."

"I was going to tell you. Before we made love that night."

"So you said. You could have told me earlier."

"I could have. I didn't think it was important. Not when I was going to leave before it became visible. And not when it meant telling you all the rest."

"I wish you had told me."

As memory of Sterling's reaction to her pregnancy came back to her, Sara lifted herself off his lap, careful this time not to put too much weight on the injured ankle.

"You say now you wish you'd known," she said abruptly.

"Yes."

"But when you heard about the pregnancy, you were so upset. You treated me like a slut, as if I'd lost all right to your respect. You *judged* me, Sterling. Do you know how hurtful that was?"

"Sara—"

"I'd fallen in love with you. I thought I knew you, that you were tolerant and understanding. You judged me, Sterling, and I couldn't bear it."

"I didn't judge you, Sara," he said.

She stared at him. "But you did! You found out I wasn't the virgin you'd taken me for, and then there was the pregnancy. You turned so cold and hostile. If it hadn't been for my ankle, I wouldn't have let you talk me into coming here with you."

"I'd have followed you, wherever you went. You don't really think I'd have let you get away from me, do you, darling? Just as I wouldn't have let you go with Larry. I would have done my damnedest to persuade you that I was the man you really loved."

"Does it matter," she said, "that I don't understand what you're saying?"

"It's true I was upset, my darling, but not for the reasons you imagined. When I heard you were pregnant— I couldn't bear the thought of you with another man. I loved you so much, I wanted to be the first.''

''That doesn't explain the way you've been treating me,'' Sara said slowly.

''It was the lack of trust that got to me. As you say, pregnancies happen all the time, and only an idiot would be judgmental. What bugged me was the fact that the woman I loved didn't trust me enough to tell me the truth about herself.''

''I think I understand,'' she said.

''Right at the beginning, I told you never to lie to me, Sara.''

''I didn't lie, Sterling.''

''By omission, you did.''

She thought about it. ''I guess you're right.''

''Let's put it all behind us now, darling. And let's make a pact never to keep secrets from each other.''

''I want that, too,'' she said fervently.

Sterling held out his arms to her, and she went willingly to his lap.

After some minutes of kissing, Sara said, ''Do you really want to be my baby's father?''

''Yes!''

''Larry's child.''

''*Our* child, darling. We can't change the fact that Larry is the biological father, but the man is out of our lives now. I'll be the only father our child will ever know.'' He searched her face. ''Will you be able to love the baby, Sara?''

''I love it already,'' she told him simply.

Putting his hand beneath her shirt, he stroked her stomach. ''I love it, too.''

''It will start moving quite soon now.''

''And I'll put my hand here and feel it.''

''Lucky child to have you as a father, Sterling.''

''I'm the lucky one, my darling. A wife and a child. It's almost too much to take in.''

He stood up, cradling her against him. "Let's get married soon."

"Oh, darling, yes!"

"Will your parents come to the wedding?"

"I think they will. I hope so! I miss them both so much."

"They must be worried sick about you."

"I called them a couple of times. And sent them letters. When I was in town, I asked tourists to mail letters for me from some other state. I didn't want them to know where I was. That way they could never be forced to give information to Larry."

"Call them tonight, Sara. Get them to come out soon. And meanwhile, we'll make arrangements for the wedding."

"Yes!"

"But not today," Sterling said. "The arrangements can wait till tomorrow. Right now, there's only one thing I want to do with you."

"I want it, too," she whispered, as he carried her out of the office and into her bedroom.

MILLS & BOON®

Makes
any time
special

Enjoy a romantic novel from
Mills & Boon®

Presents™ Enchanted™ Temptation®

Historical Romance™ Medical Romance™

MILLS & BOON®

Next Month's Romance Titles

♡

Each month you can choose from a wide variety of romance novels from Mills & Boon®. Below are the new titles to look out for next month from the Presents™ and Enchanted™ series.

Presents™

THE SPANISH GROOM	Lynne Graham
HER GUILTY SECRET	Anne Mather
THE PATERNITY AFFAIR	Robyn Donald
MARRIAGE ON THE EDGE	Sandra Marton
THE UNEXPECTED BABY	Diana Hamilton
VIRGIN MISTRESS	Kay Thorpe
MAKESHIFT MARRIAGE	Daphne Clair
SATURDAY'S BRIDE	Kate Walker

Enchanted™

AN INNOCENT BRIDE	Betty Neels
NELL'S COWBOY	Debbie Macomber
DADDY AND DAUGHTERS	Barbara McMahon
MARRYING WILLIAM	Trisha David
HIS GIRL MONDAY TO FRIDAY	Linda Miles
BRIDE INCLUDED	Janelle Denison
OUTBACK WIFE AND MOTHER	Barbara Hannay
HAVE BABY, WILL MARRY	Christie Ridgway

On sale from 7th May 1999

H1 9904

Available at most branches of WH Smith, Tesco, Asda, Martins, Borders, Easons, Volume One/James Thin and most good paperback bookshops

MILLS & BOON®

Medical Romance™

COMING NEXT MONTH

VILLAGE PARTNERS by Laura MacDonald

Dr Sara Denton tried to forget Dr Alex Mason, but it didn't work. Then she went to her uncle's and found Alex was a partner at the general practice! And Alex *really* wanted her to stay...

ONE OF A KIND by Alison Roberts

Dr Sam Marshall, fresh from Australia, was certainly unique! Sister Kate Campbell, with an A&E department to run at the busy London hospital, had no time to spare, but Sam was persistent!

MARRYING HER PARTNER by Jennifer Taylor
A Country Practice—the first of four books.

Dr Elizabeth Allen wasn't comfortable with change, but when Dr James Sinclair arrived at the Lake District practice, change was inevitable!

ONE OF THE FAMILY by Meredith Webber

Nurse Sarah Tremaine wanted to adopt baby Sam, but first she had to get permission from the child's uncle. But Dr Adam Fletcher didn't know he had a nephew...

Available from 7th May 1999

Available at most branches of WH Smith, Tesco, Asda, Martins, Borders, Easons, Volume One/James Thin and most good paperback bookshops

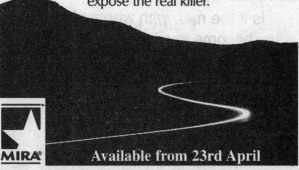

4 FREE

books and a surprise gift!

We would like to take this opportunity to thank you for reading this Mills & Boon® book by offering you the chance to take FOUR more specially selected titles from the Enchanted™ series absolutely FREE! We're also making this offer to introduce you to the benefits of the Reader Service™—

- ★ FREE home delivery
- ★ FREE gifts and competitions
- ★ FREE monthly Newsletter
- ★ Exclusive Reader Service discounts
- ★ Books available before they're in the shops

Accepting these FREE books and gift places you under no obligation to buy, you may cancel at any time, even after receiving your free shipment. Simply complete your details below and return the entire page to the address below. *You don't even need a stamp!*

YES! Please send me 4 free Enchanted books and a surprise gift. I understand that unless you hear from me, I will receive 6 superb new titles every month for just £2.40 each, postage and packing free. I am under no obligation to purchase any books and may cancel my subscription at any time. The free books and gift will be mine to keep in any case.

N9EA

Ms/Mrs/Miss/Mr ....Initials.................................
BLOCK CAPITALS PLEASE

Surname ....

Address ....

....

....Postcode.................................

Send this whole page to:
THE READER SERVICE, FREEPOST CN81, CROYDON, CR9 3WZ
(Eire readers please send coupon to: P.O. BOX 4546, DUBLIN 24.)

MILLS & BOON®

Makes any time special™

The Regency Collection

Mills & Boon® is delighted to bring back, for a limited period, 12 of our favourite Regency Romances for you to enjoy.

These special books will be available for you to collect each month from May, and with two full-length Historical Romance™ novels in each volume they are great value at only £4.99.

Volume One available from 7th May